SE

CAPTIVES OF THE FRONTIER

BY EDWARD S. ELLIS

CHAPTER I.
THE STRANGER.

The clear ring of an ax was echoing through the arches of a forest, three-quarters of a century ago; and an athletic man was swinging the instrument, burying its glittering blade deep in the heart of the mighty kings of the wood.

Alfred Haverland was an American, who, a number of years before, had emigrated from the more settled provinces in the East, to this then remote spot in western New York. Here, in the wilderness, he had reared a humble home, and, with his loving partner, and a sister, laid the foundation for a settlement. True, this "settlement" was still small, consisting only of the persons mentioned, and a beautiful blue-eyed maiden, their daughter; but Haverland saw that the tide of emigration was rolling rapidly and surely to the west, and, ere many years, the villages and cities would take the place of the wild forest, while the Indians would be driven farther on toward the setting sun.

The woodman was a splendid specimen of "nature's noblemen." His heavy coat lay upon a log a short distance away, and his swelling, ponderous chest was covered only by a close-fitting under garment, with the collar thrown open, showing the glowing neck and heaving breast. Substantial pants met the strong moccasins which encased his feet. A small raccoon-skin cap rested upon the back of his head, exposing his forehead, while his black hair swept around his shoulders. His features were regular and strongly marked. The brow was rather heavy, the nose of the Roman cast, and the eyes of a glittering blackness. So he stood with one foot thrust forward; his muscles, moving and ridging as they were called in to play, betrayed their formidable strength.

Still the flashing ax sank deeper and deeper into the oak's red heart, until it had gone clean through and met the breach upon the opposite side. Then the grand old forest king began to totter. Haverland stepped back and ran his eye to the top, as he noticed it yielding. Slowly it leaned, increasing each second, until it rushed seemingly forward, and came down to the earth with a thundering crash and rebound. He stood a moment, his hot breath issuing like steam from his chest, and then moved forward toward its branches. At that instant his trained ear detected a suspicious sound, and dropping his ax, he caught up his rifle and stood on the defensive.

"How de do? how de do? ain't frightened I hope; it's nobody but me, Seth Jones, from New Hampshire," said the new-comer in a peculiar accent. As the woodman looked up he saw a curious specimen of the genus homo before him. He is what is termed a Yankee, being from New Hampshire; but he was such a person as is rarely met with, and yet which is too often described now-a-days. He possessed a long, thin Roman nose, a small twinkling gray eye, with a lithe muscular frame, and long dangling limbs. His feet were encased in well-fitting shoes, while the rest of his dress was such as was in vogue on the frontiers at the time of which we write. His voice was in that peculiar, uncertain state, which is sometimes seen when it is said to be "changing." When excited, it made sounds singular and unimaginable.

The woodman, with characteristic penetration, read the man before him at a glance. Changing his rifle to his left hand, he extended the other.

"Certainly not, my friend; but then, you know, these are times, in which it behooves us all to use caution and prudence; and where one is placed in such a remote section as this it would be criminal to be careless, when more than one life is dependent upon me for support and protection."

2

"Very true, very true, you're right there, Mr. —— ah! I declare, I don't know your name."

"Haverland."

"You're right, as I said, Mr. Have-your-land, or Haverland as the case may be. I tell you these are dubious times—no disputin' that, and I am considerably s'prised when I heard the ring of an ax down in these parts."

"And I was equally surprised to meet your visage when I looked up. Jones, I believe you said was your name."

"Exactly:—Seth Jones, from New Hampshire. The Jones' are a numerous family up there—rather too many of them for comfort,—so I migrated. Mought be acquainted perhaps?"

"No; I have no acquaintances, to my knowledge, in that section."

"Haven't, eh? Thought the Jones' were pretty generally known through the country. Some remarkable geniuses have sprung from the family? But what under the sun keeps you out in this heathen country? What brought you here?"

"Enterprise, sir; I was tired of the civilized portion of our country, and, when such glorious fields were offered to the emigrant, as are here spread before him, I considered it a duty to avail myself of them, and I have done so. And now, sir, be equally frank with me, and let me know what induced you to visit this perilous region when you had no reason to suppose that a settlement had yet been commenced by the whites. You look to me as if you were an Indian hunter or scout."

"Wal, perhaps I am. At any rate I have been. I was scout among the Green Mountain Boys, under Colonel Allen, and staid with them till the Revolution was finished. After that, I went down on the farm and worked a while with the old man. Something occurred in our neighborhood that led me to think, it was best for me to leave, I won't say what it was, but I will say it was no crime I committed. I stopped at the settlement down the river a few days, and then come to the conclusion to take a tramp in these parts."

"I am very glad you have come, for it isn't often you get sight of a white face. I hope you will take the welcome of a backwoodsman, and make your home with us as long a time as you can—remembering that the longer you stay, the more welcome you will be."

3

"I shall probably stay till you git tired of me, at any rate," laughed the eccentric Seth Jones.

"As you are from the East, probably you can give information of the state of feeling among the Indians between that section and us. From your remarks, I should infer, however, that nothing very serious threatens."

"Don't know 'bout that," replied Seth, shaking his head and looking to the ground.

"Why so, my friend?"

"I tell you what, you, I heerd orful stories 'long the way. They say since this war, the darned red-coats have kept the Injins at work. Leastways it's pretty sartin they are at work, anyhow."

"Are you sure?" asked the woodman, betraying an anxiety in his speech.

"Purty sure. There's a little settlement down here some miles, (I have forgot the name,) sot on by the imps, and burned all up."

"Is it possible? Reports have reached me during the past three or four months, of the deadly hostility existing between the whites and reds, but I was glad to doubt it. Although, I sometimes felt it was wrong."

"'Twas so; and if you vally that ar wife of your bussum, and your little cherubims, (as I allow you've got,) you'd better be makin' tracks for safer quarters. Why, how have you stood it so long?"

"My conduct toward the Indians has ever been characterized by honesty and good will upon my part, and they have ever evinced a friendly feeling toward me, and my helpless ones. I place great reliance upon this state of feeling, in fact, my only reliance."

"Just so; but I tell you, it won't do to trust an Ingin. They're obstropertous. Go to put your finger on them, and they ain't thar. Jest so, by gracious."

"I fear there is too much truth in your suspicions," replied Haverland, in a saddened tone.

"I'm glad I've tumbled onto you, coz I begin to git skeerish, and I like to do a feller a good turn, and I'll stick to you, bein' I've found you."

"Thank you, friend, and let us now proceed homeward. I intended to spend the day in work, but your words have taken away all desire."

4

"Sorry to do it; but it's best, ain't it?"

"Certainly, it would have been wrong, had you not warned me of impending danger. Let us go home."

So saying, Alfred drew on his coat, slung his rifle and ax over his shoulder, and struck into a path in the forest, which he himself had used, and with a thoughtful tread, made his way homeward. Close behind him, followed his new-made friend.

CHAPTER II.
THE DARK CLOUD.

During the walk homeward, Haverland spoke but few words, although his loquacious friend kept up a continual, unremitting stream of talk. The woodman's heart was too heavy to join him in his humorous, pointless words. Although dark and fearful suspicions had flitted before him, he had closed his eyes upon them, until he could no longer shun them, they appeared at every turn, and now resumed a terrible certainty.

Although at the time of which we refer, the Revolutionary struggle of the colonies had closed, and their freedom was placed upon a firm basis, yet universal peace by no means reigned. Dark, sanguinary, and bloody tragedies were constantly enacted upon the frontiers for a generation afterward. The mother country, failing in her work of subjugation, continued to incite the Indians to revolting barbarities upon the unoffending inhabitants. They found them too-willing instruments, and, instigated by them, a protracted war was long maintained; and, when the moving cause was removed, the savages still continued the unequal conflict. As every one acquainted with our history must know, the war on the frontiers has been an almost interminable one. As the tide of emigration has rolled westward, it has ever met that fiery counter-surge, and only overcome it, by incessant battling and effort. And even now, as the distant shores of the Pacific are well nigh reached, that resisting wave still gives forth its lurid flashes of conflict.

In a pleasant valley, stood the humble home of Alfred Haverland. His own vigorous arm had cleared off a space on all sides, so that his residence stood at some distance from the forest, which rolled away for miles. In the clearing still remained the stumps of the fallen trees, and in some places the rich, virgin soil had been broken, and was giving signs of the exhaustless wealth it retained in its bosom, waiting only for the hand of man to bring it forth.

5

The house itself, was such as are generally found in new settlements. A number of heavy logs, placed compactly together, with an opening for a door, and one for a window, were all that could attract attention from the outside. Within, were two apartments, the lower and upper. The former was used for all purposes except that of sleeping, which, of course, was done in the upper. In building it, Haverland had made little preparations for defence, as he fondly hoped it would never be needed for such, and it seemed to him that the idea of danger would ever be before him, should he construct it thus. And, besides, should he use his utmost skill in the purpose mentioned, he knew it would avail him little. He had no means of withstanding a protracted siege, and a handful of assailants could bring him to any terms.

As he stepped forth into the clearing, Ina, his daughter, caught sight of him, and bounded out the cabin to meet him.

"Oh, father! I am glad you have come back so soon, but dinner isn't ready. Did you think it was? I was just telling mother——"

She paused suddenly, as she caught sight of a stranger, and with her hand on her mouth, stood, fearing to approach, and afraid to yield to the impulse of turning, and running into the house again.

"No, I didn't think dinner-time had come, but as I had a friend to visit me, I thought I could entertain him at home better than in the woods. But where is your kiss, dear?"

The father stooped, and touched his lips to the ruby ones of his blooming child, and taking her hand, moved forward toward the cabin.

"Whew! if that ain't a purty flower, then kick me!" exclaimed Seth Jones, in admiration. "Was she originated in these parts? Darter, I s'pose? Perhaps not, though?"

"Yes, she is my daughter, although she was not born in these parts."

"Dew tell. Darned if she ain't a beauty, and that makes what I said——"

The father motioned to him that the theme was forbidden, and they walked silently toward the house.

It was no wonder that Ina Haverland drew forth such encomiums from Seth Jones. She was, indeed, a beautiful creature. She had seen some fifteen or sixteen summers, several of which had been spent in the wilderness, which was now her home. She was rather small in stature, but graceful as a gazelle, free from the restraints which the conventionalities of life impose upon those of her age. She had dark hair, gathered in a roll behind, fine expressive blue eyes, a perfect Grecian nose, thin lips, and full chin, rendering the profile perfectly straight from the forehead downward. Her face was oval, and her complexion almost too light for a full enjoyment of health. Her dress was a semi-civilized one, consisting of a short skirt, with leggins beautifully wrought, and a loose sack, similar to the ones worn at the present day. Her small feet were encased in tiny mocassins, elaborately wrought with beads and Indian ornaments, and a string of wampum hung around the neck.

She led the way toward the house, and the three entered.

Haverland introduced his friend to his sister and wife, as a man who had chanced down in this direction, and who would probably tarry a few days. But the quick eye of his wife caught the thoughtful expression upon her husband's face, and she felt there was something yet unrevealed—something deeper and more important, that was to be disclosed. She, however, forbore questioning or hinting, knowing that he would communicate what was necessary, when he deemed the proper time had come.

A common-place conversation was maintained until the meal was prepared by the busy housewife, when they all gathered around the board. An earnest blessing was invoked upon the humble food, and it was partaken of in silence.

"Wife," said Haverland tenderly, "I will depart awhile with this friend here, and you and Mary may busy yourselves as you think best till I return. Probably I will not be back until toward night. Take no anxiety upon my account."

"I will endeavor not to, but, dear husband, go not far from home, for strange fears have come over me since morning."

Even the usually staid and calm face of Mary, betrayed an unusual expression of anxiety.

"Fear not, wife, I will not go far."

Haverland now stepped outside, where he saw Seth, all agape, gazing at Ina, as she passed to and fro in the house.

"By gracious, you, I'm goin' to fall in love with that gal. No 'bjections, hope?"

"No," answered Haverland, with a faint smile, "her heart is unfettered, and I hope it will remain so for a long time."

"Oh! I don't mean to love her as you dew yer old woman—yer wife. I mean jest as I would my darter, yer know. She's too small to think about lovyers yit. Don't you let sich a thing git inter her head for five years or more."

"I'll try not to; but let us take a walk. I have something to say, which I would that they should not know for the present."

"All right—but jest hold on a minute."

At this juncture, Ina appeared with a small vessel, as if she intended bringing some water from some spring nigh at hand.

"Hold on a minute, gal, my beauty," said Seth, stepping forward, and reaching for the pail. "That's too big a load for you to carry."

"No, I have done it often, thank you, but it is no work for me."

"But jest let me fetch it this time, if only to show my good will, and my activity."

Ina laughingly yielded the vessel, and watched him as he took long, awkward strides toward the point where the path led into the forest.

"How far is it off?" he asked, turning round, as he reached the point mentioned.

"A short distance," answered Haverland, "the path leads to it."

Seth made some unintelligible answer, as he jerked his head back and disappeared.

This simple occurrence that we have just narrated, although trivial in itself, was one of the circumstances which often controls important acts, and which seem to show that an all-wise Ruler, orders them to suit His purpose, and to bring about good in the end. Seth Jones had no object other than a little amusement in his course, yet before he returned, he saw how fortunate it was.

He strode rapidly forward, and after passing a short distance, reached the spring. As he stooped, he was sure he heard a movement in the bushes beyond; and, as he was about to dip the vessel, he saw in the smooth face of the water, a movement in the shrubbery. He had too much cunning and prudence to affect

8

knowledge of it, and he filled the vessel without betraying any signs of suspicion. As he rose to the upright position, he gave an apparently careless sweep of his vision, and not twenty feet distant he saw the crouching forms of two Indians! As he turned his back, there was a peculiar, uncomfortable feeling, as he knew that it was the easiest matter in the world to receive one or two cold bullets. He, however, quickened his step not in the least, and manifested no uneasiness, as he came to view in the clearing; and laughingly handed the water to Ina.

"Come, let us go," said Haverland, moving toward the spring.

"Not that ar way, by a long shot!" said Seth, with a meaning shake of his head.

"Why not?"

"I'll tell you purty soon."

"Let us to the river, then?"

"That'll do, 'specially as it ain't fur from your house!"

Haverland looked searchingly at him, and he saw there was a deep meaning behind these words, yet he said nothing, and led the way toward the river.

This stream was but a few hundred yards from the house, and flowed in a northerly and southerly direction. It was very smooth at this point, and not very wide, yet a mile or so farther down, it debouched into a large, broad, and deep river. The banks were lined, most of the distance, by close, impenetrable shrubbery, overreached by lofty trees, which were the edges of the almost interminable wilderness that then covered this part of the State, and of which great portions remain unto the present day.

Haverland moved to a spot where he had often stood and conversed with his wife, when they first entered the place. Resting his rifle upon the earth, and folding his arms over the muzzle, he turned around and looked Seth full in the face.

"What did you mean, by telling me not to go far from the house?"

"Jest hole on a bit," replied Seth, bending his ear as if to listen. Haverland watched him earnestly, and he also heard something unusual—as if some one were rowing a canoe in the water. His companion then stepped down to the

9

water's edge, and signalized for him to approach. Haverland did so, and looked down the river. Some hundred yards off he saw a canoe rapidly moving down stream, impelled by the oars of three Indians!

"That is what I meant," said he in a whisper, stepping back.

"Did you see them?" asked Haverland.

"I reckon I did. They were at the spring, watching for your gal to come, so that they mought run off with her."

CHAPTER III.
THE DARK CLOUD BURSTS.

"Are you certain?" asked Haverland, with a painful eagerness.

"As sure as I live!"

"How? when? where did you see them? Pray, answer quick, for I feel that the lives of precious ones stand in peril."

"The facts are few—they are. When I went down to the spring, I seed them pesky varmints thar, and I knowed they war waitin' for your little booty, 'cause if they wa'n't, they'd have walloped me thunderin' soon. I seed 'em sneaking 'round, and purtended as though I didn't 'spicion nothin'. They've found I's about, and have gone down for more help. They'll be back here tonight with a whole pack. Fact, by gracious!"

"You speak truly; and, as matters stand thus, it is time for action."

"Exactly so; and what is it you propose to dew?"

"As you have afforded me such signal aid thus far, I must again ask you for advice."

"Pshaw! don't you know what to dew, man?"

"I have a plan, but I would hear yours first."

"Wal, I can give it purty soon. You know well enough you're in tight quarters, and the best thing you can do is to git away from here a leetle quicker nor no time. You know the settlements ain't more nor twenty miles off, and you'd better pack up and be off, and lose no time, neither."

10

"That was my plan, exactly. But hold! we must go by water, and will it not be best to wait and go by night, when we will have the darkness to protect us? We have just learned that the river contains enough enemies to frustrate our designs should they be known. Yes, we must wait till night."

"You're right there; and, as there is no moon, we'll have a good chance, especially as we have to go down stream instead of up. I tell yeou, the war is going on. When I left home, I had an idee things would be fixed so as to stop these infarnal redskins from committin' on their depredations, although they looked mighty squally; but 'tain't no use, and it won't do to trust these critters."

Shortly after, Haverland turned and entered the house, followed by Seth. He called his wife and sister in, and explained, in a few words, the circumstances. It was but a realization of the fears entertained, and no time was lost in useless laments. Preparations were immediately made for the removal. The woodman owned a large boat, somewhat similar to the flat-boats seen at this day upon the western waters. This was hauled in beneath the shrubbery which overhung the bank, and into this their things were placed. During the removal Seth remained along the river-bank, keeping watch of the stream, lest their enemies might return unawares.

The removal occupied most of the afternoon, and it was not until the shadows were lengthening across the river, that the last article was placed on board. This completed, all seated themselves in the boat, and waited for the rapidly approaching darkness, to glide out into the stream.

"It is hard," said Haverland, somewhat moodily, "to leave one's home after all the difficulty in rearing it is finished."

"Fact, by gracious!" added Seth, whom Mary eyed very closely, as if not satisfied with the fellow's ways and looks.

"But it is best, dear husband. Let us hope, now, that the war is ended, and that, as we have passed through as great dangers as those that now threaten us, the time is not far distant when we may return to this spot with safety."

"We can but die once," said Mary, abstractedly, "and I am ready for any fate."

Seth studied her face with a quick, keen glance, then smiled, and said: "Oh, you look a here, now. I am captain here, by your leave, my dears, and I ain't goin' to allow any sick stomachs in this here crew." His sunny face seemed greatly to encourage the little band.

11

"I wouldn't fear to remain here now," said Ina, bravely; "I am sure we soon may return. I feel it."

Haverland kissed his child, but made no further reply, and all relapsed into a stillness, and ceased further conversation. There was something in the gathering gloom around, something in the peculiar situation in which they were placed, that imparted a despondency to all. The boat was still fastened to the shore, and the time for loosening it was close at hand. Mrs. Haverland had passed within the rude cabin, the door of which remained open, while Seth and the husband remained in the stern. Ina sat near at hand, and had fallen into the same silence that rested upon the others.

"Doesn't it look dark and awful back there?" she asked, in a whisper, of Seth, pointing toward the shore.

"It does somewhat, I think."

"And yet I wouldn't be afraid to go back to the house."

"You'd better stay in the boat, young 'un."

"You think I am afraid, do you?" she said, bounding out the boat to the shore.

"Ina! Ina! what do you mean?" asked the father, sternly.

"Oh, nothing; only I want to take a little run to ease my limbs."

"Come back here instantly!"

"Yes—oh, father! quick! quick! come take me!"

"Seize the oar and shove out!" commanded Seth, springing into the water, and shoving the boat off.

"But, for God's sake, my child!"

"You can't help her—the Injins have got her. I see 'em; drop quick, they're goin' to fire! Look out!"

At that instant there was the sharp crack of several rifles from the shore, and several tongues of fire flamed from the darkness, and the wild yell of a number of Indians pealed out in horrid strength.

12

Had it not been for Seth all would have been lost. He comprehended every thing in an instant, and saved the others.

"Oh, father! mother! The Indians have got me!" came in agonized accents from the shore.

"Merciful God! must I see my child perish without heeding her cry?" groaned Haverland, in spirit.

"No, they won't hurt her, and we must take care of ourselves while we can. Don't stand up, for they can see you."

"Father, will you leave me?" came again in heart-rending tones.

"Don't be scart, young 'un," called out Seth; "keep up a good heart. I'll git you agin ef you behave yourself. I will, as sure as I am Seth Jones. Just keep up pluck, little one." The last words were shouted loudly, for the boat was fast gliding into the stream.

The mother had heard all, and said nothing. She comprehended it, and with a groan sank back upon a seat. Mary's eyes flashed like a tigress at bay; and she did not cease to cast looks of indignation at Seth, for leaving the child to her horrid fate so coolly. But she said nothing—was as quiet and pale as a statue. Seth eyed her like a lynx; his eyeballs seemed like fire. But he was as cool as if at his ease perfectly; and he quickly made all feel that he was born for such appalling emergencies.

They were now within the center of the stream, and moving quite rapidly. The darkness was so great that the shores were now vailed from sight. And with hearts in as deep a gloom the fugitives floated downward.

CHAPTER IV.
THE LOST HOME AND A FOUND FRIEND.

It was on the morning of the day which we have just seen close. As will be remembered the air was clear and the day one of the most beautiful and pleasant of the year. The air was perfectly still, and had that peculiar, bracing sharpness, which is only felt when it is in a perfect state of rest. It was such a morning as would make every healthy person feel that to merely live was pleasure.

That part of the State of New York in which the first scenes of this life drama are laid, was a country at this time cut up and diversified by numerous streams—the greater number of comparatively small size, but a few of considerable magnitude. Skirting and between these were thousands of acres of thick luxuriant forest, while in some places were plains of great extent entirely devoid of timber.

It was about the middle of the day referred to, that a single horseman was slowly skirting one of these open patches of country, a few miles distant from Haverland's home. A mere glance would have shown that he had come a great distance, and both he and the animal he bestrode were jaded and well-nigh worn out. He was a young man, some twenty or twenty-five years of age, attired in the costume of a hunter; and, although fatigued with his long ride, the watchfulness of his motions would have shown any one that he was no stranger to frontier life. He was rather prepossessing in appearance—had fine dark eyes, curly hair and whiskers, an expressive Roman nose, and small and finely formed mouth. In front, a long polished rifle rested across the saddle ready for use at a second's warning. His horse's sides were steaming and foamy, and the animal made his way along with painfully evident weariness.

As the day waned, the traveler looked about him with more interest and eagerness. He carefully examined the streams he crossed, and the pieces of woods, as though searching for some landmark or habitation. At length he manifested a pleasure in what he saw, as though the signs were as he wished, and hurried the lagging steps of his animal.

"Yes," said he to himself, "the woodman's house can not be far from this. I remember this stream, and that wood yonder. I shall then be able to reach it by night. Come, my good horse, go ahead with better spirits, for you are near your journey's end."

A short time after, he crossed a small stream that dashed and foamed over its rocky bed, and entered the broad tract which led to the clearing in front of Haverland's door. But although he had a tolerably correct idea of his situation, he had sadly miscalculated the distance. It was already dusk when he struck the stream several miles above where we have seen the fugitives take it. This river, or creek, he knew led directly by the cabin he was seeking, and he determined to keep it until he had reached his destination. His progress was now quite tardy, from being often obliged to pass around the thick undergrowth which lined the river; and, when he reached a point that he knew was a mile distant from Haverland's cabin, it was far in the night.

"Come, my good horse, we have had a longer tramp than I expected, but we are now very near the termination of our journey. Heigh! what does that mean?"

14

The last exclamation, or question, was caused by seeing directly ahead of him, a bright lurid glare shot high into the heavens.

"Can it be that the woodman's house is fired? Impossible! and yet that is the precise spot. Heavens! something is wrong!"

Agitated by strong and painful emotions, Everard Graham (such was his name) now hurried his horse toward the spot from which the light emanated. In a short time he had proceeded as far as he dared with his horse, then dismounting, he tied him, and made his way cautiously forward on foot. The light was so strong that he found it necessary to pick his way with the greatest care.

A few moments sufficed to show him all.

He saw the house of Haverland, the one in which he expected to pass the night, but one mass of flame. And around it were a score of dark forms, leaping and dancing, and appearing in the ghastly light, like fiends in a ghostly revel.

Graham stood a moment spell-bound with horror and amazement. He expected to see the reeking bodies of Haverland and his family, or hear their groans of agony; but, as he continued gazing, he became convinced that they were either slain or had escaped, as there were no signs of their presence. He could not think they had escaped, and was compelled to believe they had been tomahawked, and perished in the flames.

It was a ghastly and almost unearthly sight—the small cabin, crackling and roaring in one mass of living flame, throwing strange shadows across the clearing, and lighting up the edges of the forest with a brightness almost as great as the sun at noonday—the score of dusky beings, leaping and shouting in wild exultation, and the vast wilderness, shutting down like an ocean of darkness around.

Gradually the flames lessened, and the woods seemed to retreat into the gloom; the shouts of the savages ceased, and they too, disappeared; and the building, which hitherto was a mass of crackling fire, was now a heap of slumbering coals and embers, which glowed with a hot redness in the darkness.

An hour or two afterward, a shadowy form could have been seen gliding stealthily and silently around the glowing ruins. He appeared like a specter as seen by the reflected light of the slumbering coals, or might have been taken for the shadow of some ruin of the building. At intervals, he paused and listened, as though he half expected to hear the footfall of some one, and then again continued his ghostly march around the ruins. Several times he stopped and

15

peered into the embers, as though he supposed the whitened bones of some human being would greet his vision, and then he recoiled and stood as if in deep and painful thought. It was Everard Graham, searching for the remains of Haverland and his family.

"I see nothing," he said musingly, "and it may be that they have escaped, or perhaps their bodies are now cooking in that heap of coals, and yet something tells me that they are not. And if it is not thus, what can have become of them? How could they have eluded the malignant vengeance of their savage foes? Who could have warned them? Ah, me! in spite of the unaccountable hope which I feel, my own sense tells me, that there are no grounds for it. Sad is the fate of the unprotected at this time."

"Fact, by gracious!"

Graham started as though he had been shot, and gazed around. A few yards off he could just discover the outlines of a man, standing as if he were contemplating himself.

"And who are you?" he asked, "that appears upon this spot at such a time?"

"I am Seth Jones, from New Hampshire. Who mought be you that happens down in these parts at this pertickler time?"

"Who am I? I am Everard Graham, a friend of the man whose house is in ruins, and who, I fear, has been slaughtered with his family."

"Exactly so; but don't speak so loud. There mought be others about, you know. Jist let's step back here where 'taint likely we'll be observed."

The speaker retreated into the darkness, while Graham followed him. At first he had had some slight misgivings, but the tones and voice of the stranger reassured him, and he followed him without distrust or hesitation.

"You say you're a friend of Haverland's, eh?" asked Seth in a whisper.

"I am, sir; I was acquainted with him before he moved out in these parts. He was an intimate friend of my father's, and I promised to pay him a visit as soon as I could possibly do so, and I am here for that purpose."

"Jest so, but you took a rayther ticklish time for it, I reckon."

"So it seems; but, if I wished to wait till it would be perfectly safe, I am afraid my visit would never be made."

"Fact, by gracious!"

"But allow me to ask whether you know any thing of the family?"

"I reckon that, perhaps, it mought be possible I do, seeing as how I've been around these times."

"Are they slain, or captives?"

"Neyther."

"Is it possible they have escaped?"

"Jest so, I helped 'em off myself."

"Thank heaven! Where are they?"

"Down the river at one of the settlements."

"How far distant is it?"

"A dozen miles, p'raps, though it mought be more, and then agin it mightn't."

"Well, let us then hasten to them, or, let me at least, as I have nothing to detain me here."

"I'm willing," said Seth, moving forward, "but I forgot to tell you the darter's 'mong the Indians, I didn't think of that."

Graham started, for, perhaps, the shrewd reader has already suspected he had more than a passing interest in the fate of Ina. Visions of a fair childish face had haunted him, and his perilous journey was owing much to their enchantment. He had played with her in childhood, and while they were yet children, they had separated; but they had pledged their hearts to each other, and looked hopefully forward to a reunion in later years. Graham had dreamed of this meeting a long time; and, now that it was so cruelly thwarted, he felt agonized indeed. Years before, when still a boy, although quite a large one, he had visited this section, and the memory of that visit had ever been a bright dream in the past. He mastered his emotion in a moment, with a strong effort, and asked his companion calmly—

"What tribe has captured Ina?"

"Them infarnal Mohawks, I believe."

"How long ago did it occur?"

"Only a few hours, as you can see by them coals there."

"Will you be kind enough to give me the particulars?"

"Sartinly."

And thereupon, Seth proceeded to narrate the incidents given in the preceding chapter, adding, however, that the parents and sister were safe. He had accompanied them himself down to the settlement mentioned, where, leaving them, he had made all haste back again, and had arrived just in time to meet Graham. At first he said he mistook him for a savage, and as he was alone, he came very near shooting him; but, as he heard him communing with himself he discovered at once that he was a white man.

"And what has brought you back here?" asked Graham, when he had finished.

"That's a pooty question to ax me, I swow! What has brought me back here? Why, the same thing, I cac'late as has brought you—to find out what is to be found out 'bout Ina, that purty darter."

"Ah—pardon me, friend, I am glad to hear it, and I am free to confess that that inducement has had more in bringing me here than any thing else. From your starting alone to rescue her, I presume you entertained hopes of recovering her, and, as you, alone, entertained such hopes, I judge there is greater room for them, when another one joins you."

"Did I say, stranger, I 'spected to git that gal again?" asked Seth in a low tone.

"You did not say so in words, it is true; but from what you said, I judged such was your intention. Was I mistaken?"

"No, sir; that's what I meant."

"I see no reason why we should not be friends, as we are both actuated by a desire to rescue an unfortunate one from the horrors of Indian captivity, and I trust, without that fact, we would find nothing distasteful in each other."

18

"Them's my sentiments, 'zactly. Give us your hand."

The two closed hands with a true friendly grip, and could each have seen the other's face in the darkness, he would have beheld a radiant expression of friendship. They then retired further into the wood and continued the conversation.

We may remark in this place, that the Indians who had captured Ina, were, as Seth had remarked, members of the Mohawk tribe. This tribe itself, was a member of the "Five Nations," including with them, the Seneca, Cayuga, Onondaga, and Oneida tribes, which have become quite famous in history. They are known among the French as the Iroquois, and among the Dutch as Maquas, while at home they are called the Mingoes, or Agamuschim, signifying the United People. The Mohawks, or Wabingi, first existed separately and alone. The Oneidas then joined them, and these in turn, were followed by the Onondagas, Senecas, and Cayugas. In the beginning of the last century, the Tuscaroras of the South, joined them, after which time they took the name of the Six Nations, although to this day, they are also known as the Five Nations. Of course, they were all united, and war made upon one tribe, was made upon all. They were truly a formidable confederation, and the Revolution testifies to what deeds they were sufficient when instigated by the British. During the predatory warfare which long existed upon the Old Frontier, the white settlers relied mainly upon stratagem to outwit their foes, and it was by this means alone that Seth Jones hoped to rescue Ina from their hands.

CHAPTER V.
ON THE TRAIL, AND A SUDDEN DEPARTURE FROM IT BY SETH.

"The Mohawks, you say, have then captured her?" remarked Graham, after a moment's pause.

"Yes; I know it's them."

"Did you get a glimpse of them?"

"I came up as soon as possible, and they were leaving at that moment. I saw one or two of them, and know'd it was them, sure 'nough. Howsumever, that don't make no difference, whether it's the Mohawks, Oneidas, or any of them blasted Five Nation niggers. They are all a set of skunks, and one would just as lief run off with a man's gal, as not. There ain't any difference atwixt 'em."

"I suppose not. The same difficulties would have to be surmounted in each case. The point is not whether one shall make an attempt at a rescue, but how shall it be done. I confess I am in a maze. The Mohawks are an exceedingly cunning people."

"That's a fact, that needn't be disputed."

"But then, you know, if we outwit them, we will not be the first whites who have done such a thing in their day!"

"That's a fact, too. Now, just hold on a minute, while I think."

Graham ceased talking for a moment, while Seth remained as if in deep and anxious thought. Suddenly lifting up his head, he remarked.

"I have it."

"Have what? The plan which must be pursued by us?"

"I cac'late I have."

"Well, out with it."

"Why, it's this. We've got to git that gal, an' no mistake."

Despite the gloominess which had been upon Graham, he could not help laughing outright at the serious tone in which this was uttered.

"What are you laughing at?" indignantly demanded Seth.

"Why, I thought we had arrived at that conclusion long since."

"I didn't think of that; so we did. Howsumever, I've thort further—hey, what's that off yonder? 'Nuther building burning?"

Graham gazed in the direction indicated, and saw that day was breaking. This he remarked to his companion.

"Yes; so 'tis, and I'm glad of it, for we want some light on this subject."

In a short time, the sun appeared above the forest, and poured a flood of golden light over the woods and streams. Birds were singing their morning songs in every part of the wood, and every thing wore as gay a look, as though

20

no deed of blood had been committed during the night. As soon as it was sufficiently light, Seth and Graham made their way toward the stream.

"As we shall shortly start," remarked the latter, "I will attend to my horse, which I brought with me. He is not a short distance away, and I will be back in a moment."

So saying, he departed in the wood. He found his horse, completely worn out, asleep upon the ground. He unloosened his fastening, and as there was abundant provender around, in the shape of young and tender twigs and luxuriant grass, he removed the saddle and bridle, and concluded to allow him free scope of the wood until his return, trusting to the rather doubtful chances of ever recovering him again. This done, he returned to his companion.

He found Seth leaning upon his rifle, and gazing meditatively into the silent stream flowing before him. Graham looked curiously at him a moment, and then said:—

"I am ready, Seth, if you are."

The individual addressed, turned without a word and strode toward the clearing. When the ruins of the house were reached, they both halted, and in an undertone, he said:

"Hunt up the trail."

Each bent his head toward the ground, and moved in a circle around the clearing. Suddenly Graham paused, and proceeding quickly several yards in the wood, halted and exclaimed:

"Here it is, Seth."

The latter hastened to his side, and stooping a moment, and running his eye along the ground, both forward and backward, replied:

"This is the trail! They ain't very keerful 'bout it now, but I reckon it'll make us open our peepers wider to see it, after we get into the wood."

"Well, as the starting point is now reached, we must perfect our arrangements. You must take the lead in following this up."

"Can't you?" asked Seth, looking up in his eyes.

"Not as well as you. From what little I have seen of you, I am sure you excel me in the knowledge of the forest. I have had some experience in fighting, but very little in tracing a foe through such a wilderness as this."

"Don't say? That's just where you 'n I disagree. I was always the one to track the tories or red-coats for old Colonel Allen, and I remember one time— but I guess I won't go to telling stories now, being as I haven't much time; but I can say, though pr'aps I oughn't to, that I can foller any red-skin as far as he can go, and I don't care how much pains he takes to cover up his tracks. You see, if I undertake to foller this, I've got to keep my nose down to the ground, and won't be likely to see any danger we're running into: that'll have to be your business. You just hang close to my heels, and keep yer eyes travellng all over."

"I'll endeavor to do my part, although I shall expect some aid from you."

"I may give some, as I can tell purty near about when the imps have gone over the tracks I'm looking at. And now we must start. I promised Haverland that I wouldn't show myself again, until I could tell him something about his darter, and I swow, I won't. Come ahead!"

With these words, Seth started ahead on a rapid walk. He was slightly inclined forward, and his keen gray eye was bent with a searching look upon the ground. Graham followed him a few feet distant, with the barrel of his rifle resting in the hollow of his left arm, while the stock was held in his right so as to be ready at a moment's warning.

The signs that led Seth Jones forward were faint, and to an ordinary observer, invisible. The Indians, although they had little fears of pursuit, were yet too cunning and experienced to neglect any caution that would mislead what enemies might be disposed to follow them. They traveled in Indian file, each one stepping in the track of the one before him, so that, judging from the tracks made, it would appear that but a single savage had been journeying in these parts. Ina was compelled to walk in this matter, and more than once when she inadvertently made a misstep, a cruel blow warned her of her task.

Sometimes the leaves, as they lay, appeared perfectly devoid of the slightest depression or disturbance, yet, had one stooped and carefully scrutinized the ground, he would have seen the faint outlines of a moccasin defined upon it, or observed that a leaf had been displaced, or perhaps a slender twig had not yet recovered the position from which it had been forced by the passing of human feet. All these were trifling indications, it is true, yet they were unerring ones to the practiced eye of the hunter, and as plain as the footprints upon the dusty roads. Soon Seth paused, and raising his head, turned toward Graham.

"We are gaining on 'em."

"Ah—are we? Glad to hear it. When is it probable we shall overtake them?"

"Can't exactly say, but not for a considerable time yet. They are tramping at a purty good gate, and they only halted last night to rest Iny now and then. Darn 'em! she'll wan't rest, I cac'late, more'n once afore she's done with 'em."

"Can't you conjecture their number?"

"There's somewhere in the neighborhood of twenty of the best warriors of the Mohawks. I can tell that by their tracks."

"How is that? They make but a single one, do they?"

"Of course not, but I rayther cac'late they make that a little different, fur all that, from what one would. Are you hungry?"

"Not at all, I can stand it till noon, without the least inconvenience."

"So can I; keep a good look-out, and now ahead again."

With these words, Seth again plunged in to the woods, and the two prosecuted their journey much as before. The sun was now high in the heavens, and its warm rays pierced the arches of the forest at many points, and there were golden patches of light scattered over the travelers' path. Several times they crossed small, sparkling streams, where sometimes could be seen signs of the pursued having slaked their thirst, and more than once the frightened deer bounded ahead, and paused and gazed in wonder at them, then leaped away again. Graham could hardly resist the temptation of bringing one of them down, especially as he began to feel a desire to taste them; but he too well knew the danger of risking a shot, when it might bring down their most mortal enemies in a moment upon them.

All at once, Seth halted and raised his hand.

"What does this mean?" he asked, gazing off in a side direction from the trail.

"What is it?" queried Graham, approaching him.

"The trail divides here. They must have separated, though I can't see what has made them."

"Isn't it a stratagem of theirs to mislead pursuers?"

23

"I believe it is! Here, you follow the main trail, while I take the side one, and we'll soon see."

Graham did as directed, although it cost him considerable trouble to perform his part. It proved as they expected. In a short time, the two trails united again.

"We must look out for such things," remarked Seth. "I've got to watch the ground closer, and you must look out that I don't pitch heels over head into a nest of the hornets."

They now proceeded cautiously and rapidly forward. About the middle of the afternoon, they halted beside a stream of considerable size. Seth produced a quantity of dried venison, which he had brought with him from the settlement, and of this they made a hearty meal. This done, they arose and again proceeded upon their journey.

"See there!" said Seth, pointing to the middle of the stream. "Do you see that stone there? Notice how it is marked, and observe that print of a moccasin beside it. One of their number has slipped off of it. Let us be keerful."

He stepped into the water, and made his way carefully across, followed by Graham. When they stepped upon dry land again, the shades of evening were gathering over the forest, and already the birds had ceased their songs. There was, however, a bright moon,—in fact, so bright, that they determined to keep up their pursuit.

The progress was now necessarily tardy, as it required the utmost straining of Seth's vision to keep the trail, and had it not been for the friendly openings in the wood, where it was as plain as at mid-day, they would have been compelled to abandon it altogether until the morning. Several times, Graham was compelled to stand, while Seth, almost on his hands and knees, searched out the "signs." They came across no evidence of the Indians having encamped, and judged from this, that they either intended reaching their tribe before doing so, or that they were somewhere in the vicinity. The latter was the most probable supposition, and prudence, demanded them to be cautious and deliberate in their movements.

Suddenly Graham noticed the woods appeared to be growing thinner and lighter in front, as though an opening was at hand. He called the attention of Seth to this, who remarked that it was very probable. In a few moments they heard a noise as of flowing water, and immediately after stood upon the bank of a large creek, or more properly a river. The current was quite rapid, yet without much hesitation, they plunged boldly in and swam across. The night being warm

24

and moderate, they suffered little inconvenience from their wet and clinging clothes, as the exercise of walking kept them sufficiently warm.

As they ascended the bank, they stood upon a vast and treeless plain over which the trail led.

"Must we cross this?" asked Graham.

"I don't see any other way. There ain't any chance to skirt it, 'cause it appears to run up and down about four thousand three hundred miles, while you can see the other side."

This was true—that is the latter part of his assertion. The plain before them, from all appearances, was a prairie of great length, but comparatively narrow breadth. The dark line of the woods upon the opposite side could be plainly seen, and did not appear more than a good hour's walk away.

"I don't see any other way," repeated Seth, musingly to himself. "It's got to be crossed, although it's a ticklish business, I swow!"

"Would it be better to wait until morning?" asked Graham.

"Why so?"

"We may walk into danger without seeing it, in the night."

"And how do you s'pose we're going to walk over here in daylight, without being targets for all the Ingins that are a mind to crack away at us?"

"Can we not pass around it?"

"Stars and garters! hain't I told you it reaches five thousand miles each way, and it would take us three years to get half-way round?"

"I was not aware that you had given me such interesting information, until just now; but, as such is the case, of course nothing is left for us but to move forward, without losing time talking."

"The trail goes purty straight," said Seth, turning and looking at the ground, "and I've no doubt it heads straight across to the other end. Hope so, 'cause it'll be convenient."

"You must help me keep watch," said Graham, "you will not need to watch the ground all the time, and you will need to keep a look out elsewhere."

As might naturally be supposed, our two friends, although quite experienced backwoodsmen, had miscalculated the distance to the opposite side of the prairie. It was full midnight, ere they reached its margin.

All was as silent as death, as they cautiously and stealthily entered the wood again. Not a breath of wind stirred the boughs on the tree-tops, and the soft murmur of the river had long died away into silence. There were a few flying clouds that obscured the moon at intervals, and rendered its light uncertain and treacherous. Seth still pressed forward. They had gone a few hundred yards, when they heard voices! Cautiously and silently they still picked their way, and soon saw the light of fire, reflected against the uppermost limbs of the trees. The fire itself was invisible, although it could not be far distant. Seth whispered for Graham to remain quiet, while he moved forward. He then stepped carefully ahead, and soon reached a massive natural embankment, up which on his hands and knees he crawled. He peered carefully over this and saw, down in a sort of hollow, the whole Indian encampment! There were over twenty gathered around, most of whom were extended upon the ground asleep, while several sat listlessly smoking and gazing into the fire. Seth looked but a moment, as he knew there were watchful sentinels, and it was fortunate that he had not been discovered, as it was. Carefully retreating, he made his way down again to Graham.

"What's the news?" asked the latter.

"—sh! not so loud. They're all there."

"She, too?"

"I s'pose, though I didn't see her."

"What do you intend doing?"

"I don't know. We can't do nothin' to-night; it's too near morning. If we could git her, we couldn't get a good 'nough start to give us a chance. We've got to wait till to-morrow night. There's a lot of 'em on the watch too. We've got to lay low till daylight, and foller 'long behind 'em."

The two made their way off in a side direction, so as not to be likely to attract notice in the morning, should any of the savages take the back trail. Here they remained until daylight.

26

They heard the Indians, as soon as it was fully light, preparing their morning meal; and, as they deemed they could see them without incurring great peril, they determined to obtain a glimpse of them, in order to assure themselves whether Ina was among them or not. Each had suspicion the company had separated, and that their trail had been overlooked in the darkness.

Accordingly, the two crept noiselessly to the top. There was a heavy, peculiar sort of brier growing on the summit of the embankment, which was fortunately so impenetrable as to effectually conceal their bodies. Seth pressed against this and peered over. His head just came above the undergrowth, and he could plainly see all that was transpiring. Graham, with an unfortunate want of discretion, placed his arm on Seth's shoulder, and gazed over him! Yet singularly enough, neither was seen. Graham was just in the act of lowering his head, when the briers, which were so matted together as to hold the pressure against them like a woven band, gave way, and Seth rolled like a log down the embankment, directly among the savages!

CHAPTER VI.
A RUN FOR LIFE.

When the sad event just chronicled took place, and Seth made a rather unceremonious entrance into view of the savages, Graham felt that he too was in peril, and his life depended upon his own exertions. To have offered resistance would have been madness, as there were full thirty Indians at hand. Flight was the only resource left, and without waiting to see the fate of Seth, our hero made a bound down the embankment, alighting at the bottom, and struck directly across the plain, toward the timber that lined the river. He had gained several hundred yards, when several prolonged yells told him that he was discovered, and was a flying fugitive. Casting his eye behind him, he saw five or six Indians already down the embankment and in full chase.

And now commenced a race of life and death. Graham was as fleet of foot as a deer, and was well-trained and disciplined, but his pursuers numbered five of the swiftest runners of the Mohawk nation, and he feared he had at last found his match. Yet he was as skillful and cunning as he was sinewy and fleet of foot. The plain over which he was speeding was perfectly bare and naked for six or eight miles before him, while it stretched twice that distance on either hand, before the slightest refuge was offered. Thus, it will be seen, he took the only course which offered hope—a dead run for it, where the pursuer and pursued possessed equal advantages.

He was pretty certain that his pursuers possessed greater endurance than himself, and that in a long run he stood small chance of escape, while in a short race he believed he could distance any living Indian. So he determined to try the speed of his enemies.

As he heard their yells, he bounded forward almost at the top of his speed. The pursuers, however, maintained the same regular and rapid motion. Graham continued his exertions for about half a mile, making such use of his arms and limbs as to give the impression that he was doing his utmost. Toward the latter part of the first mile, his speed began to slacken, and his dangling limbs and furtive glances behind him, would have convinced any one that he was nigh exhausted.

But this was only a stratagem, and it succeeded as well as he could have wished. The Indians believed that he had committed a common and fatal error—that of calling into play the utmost strength and speed of which he was master at the outset, and that he was now wearied out, while they themselves were just warming into the glow of the chase. Seeing this, each sent up a shout of exultation, and darted ahead at the top of his speed, each endeavoring to reach and tomahawk him before his companion.

But their surprise was unbounded when they saw the fugitive shoot ahead with the velocity of a race-horse, while his veins, too, were only filling with the hot blood of exertion. They saw this and they saw, too, that should such speed continue long, he would be far beyond their reach, and all now ran as they never ran before.

We say Graham's stratagem succeeded. It did, and it gave him the knowledge he wished. It showed him that he had met his match! His pursuers, at least one or two of them, were nearly as fleet as was he; and, although he might distance them for a time, yet ere half the race was finished he would inevitably lose the vantage ground!

Could one have stood and gazed upon this race of life, he would have seen a thrilling scene. Far ahead, over a vast plain, a fugitive white man was flying, and his swift steady gait showed that his limbs were well-trained and were now put to their severest test. As his feet doubled with such quickness beneath him as to be almost invisible, the ground glided like a panorama from under them.

Behind were a half-dozen savages, their gleaming visages distorted with the passions of exultation, vengeance, and doubt, their garments flying in the wind, and their strength pressed to its utmost bounds. They were scattered at different distances from each other, and were spreading over the prairie, so as to cut off the fugitive's escape in every direction.

Two Indians maintained their places side by side, and it was evident that the pursuit would soon be left to them. The others were rapidly falling behind, and were already relaxing their exertions. Graham saw the state of things, and it thrilled him with hope. Could he not distance these also? Would they not leave him in such a case? And could he not escape ere he was compelled to give out from exhaustion?

"At any rate I will try, and God help me!" he uttered, prayerfully, shooting ahead with almost superhuman velocity. He glanced back and saw his followers, and they seemed almost standing still, so rapidly did he leave them behind.

But as nature compelled him to again cease the terrific rate at which he was going, he saw his unwearied pursuers again recovering their lost ground. The parties now understood each other. The Indians saw his maneuvers, and avoided the trap, and kept on in the same unremitting relentless speed, fully certain that this would sooner or later compel him to yield; while Graham knew that the only chance of prolonging the contest rested in his dropping into and continuing his ordinary speed.

They now sunk into the same steady and terribly monotonous run. Mile after mile flew beneath them, and still so exact and similar were their relative rates, that they were absolutely stationary with regard to each other! The two Indians now remained alone, and they were untiring—they were determined that they should continue to the end!

At last Graham saw the friendly timber but a short distance from him. The trees seemed beckoning him to their friendly shelter, and panting and gasping he plunged in among them—plunged right ahead till he stood upon the bank of a large, rapidly-flowing stream.

When the Anglo-Saxon's body is pitted against that of the North American Indian, it sometimes yields; but when his mind takes the place of contestant, it never loses.

Graham gazed hurriedly around him, and in the space of a dozen seconds his faculties had wrought enough for a lifetime—wrought enough to save him.

Throwing his rifle aside, he waded carefully into the stream until he stood waist deep. Then sinking upon his face, he swam rapidly upward until he had gone a hundred yards. Here he struck vigorously out into the channel, swimming up stream as well as across it, so as not to reach the bank at a lower point. The current was very swift, and required an exhausting outlay of his already fainting frame before he reached the opposite shore. Here he immediately sprang upon the shore, ran quickly a short distance down the stream, making his trail as plain as possible; and then springing into the stream, swam rapidly upward, remaining as close to the shore as possible, so as to avoid the resisting current. The reason of these singular movements will soon be plain.

The shore was lined by thickly overhanging bushes, and after swimming until he supposed it time for his pursuers to come up, he glided beneath their friendly shelter, and awaited for the further development of things. Almost immediately after, both appeared upon the opposite bank, but at a point considerably lower down. Without hesitation, they sprang into the stream and swam across. As they landed, they commenced a search, and a yell announced the discovery of the trail. Instantly after, another yell proclaimed their disappointment, as they lost it in the river.

The savages supposed that the fugitive had again taken to the water, and had either drowned or reached the other side. At any rate, they had lost what they considered a certain prey, and with feelings of baffled malignity they sullenly swam back again, searched the other side an hour or so, and then took their way back to their companions.

CHAPTER VII.
THE EXPERIENCE OF SETH.
"By gracious! stars and garters! &c.! &c.! This is a new way of introducing one's self!" exclaimed Seth, as he sprawled out among the savages around the council fire.

The consternation of the Indians at this sudden apparition among them may well be imagined. The crackling of the undergrowth above, had aroused them, yet the advent of Seth was so sudden and almost instantaneous, that ere they could form a suspicion of the true nature of things, he was among them. Their habitual quickness of thought came to them at once. Graham was seen as he wheeled and fled, and as has been shown, a number sprang at once in pursuit, while a dozen leaped upon Seth, and as many tomahawks were raised.

"Now jest hold on," commanded Seth; "there ain't any need of being in a hurry. Plenty time to take my hair. Fact, by gracious."

His serio-comical manner arrested and amused his captors. They all paused and looked at him, as if expecting another outburst, while he contented himself with gazing at them with a look of scornful contempt. Seeing this, one sprang forward, and clenching his hair in a twist, hissed—

"Oh! cuss Yankee! we burn him!"

"If you know what's best, ole chap, you'll take yer paw off my head in a hurry. Ef you don't you mought find it rather convenient to."

The savage, as if to humor him, removed his hand, and Seth's rifle too. Seth gazed inquiringly at him a moment, and then with an air of conscious superiority, said:

"I'll lend that to you awhile, provided you return it all right. Mind, you be keerful now, 'cause that ar gun cost something down in New Hampshire."

From what has just been written, it will doubtless be suspected that Seth's conduct was a part which he was playing. When thrown into peril by the impatience of his companion, he saw at once that an attempt at flight was useless. Nothing was left but to submit to his misfortune with the best grace possible; and yet there was a way in which this submission could be effected which would result better for himself than otherwise. Had he offered resistance, or submitted despairingly, as many a man would have done, he would doubtless have been tomahawked instantly. So, with a readiness of thought, which was astonishing, he assumed an air of reckless bravado. This, as we have shown, had the desired result thus far. How it succeeded after, will be seen in the remaining portion of this history.

Seth Jones was a man whose character could not be read in an hour, or day. It required a long companionship with him to discover the nicely shaded points, and the characteristics which seemed in many cases so opposite. United with a genial, sportive humor and apparent frankness, he was yet far-seeing and cautious, and could read the motives of a man almost at a glance. With a countenance which seemed made expressly to veil his soul, his very looks were deceptive; and, when he chose to play a certain role, he could do it to perfection. Had one seen him when the conversation above recorded took place, he would have unhesitatingly set him down as a natural-born idiot.

"How you like to burn, eh, Yankee?" asked a savage, stooping and grinning horribly in his face.

"I don't know; I never tried it," replied Seth with as much nonchalance as though it was a dinner to which he was referring.

"E-e-e-e! you will try it, Yankee."

"Don't know, yet; there are various opinions about that p'raps. When the thing is did I mought believe it."

"You, sizzle nice—nice meat—good for burn!" added another savage, grasping and feeling his arm.

"Just please to not pinch, my friend."

The savage closed his fingers like iron rods, and clenched the member till Seth thought it would be crushed. But, though the pain was excruciating, he manifested not the least feeling. The Indian tried again and again, till he gave up and remarked, expressive of his admiration of the man's pluck.

"Good Yankee! stand pinch well."

"Oh! you wan't pinching me, was you? Sorry I didn't know it. Try again, you mought p'raps do better."

The savage, however, retired, and another stepped forward and grasped the captive's hand.

"Soft, like squaw's hand—let me feel it," he remarked, shutting his own over it like a vice. Seth winced not in the least; but, as the Indian in turn was about to relinquish his attempt at making sport for his comrades, Seth said:

"Your paws don't appear very horny," and closed over it with a terrific grip. The savage stood it like a martyr, till Seth felt the bones of his hand actually displacing, and yielding like an apple. He determined, as he had in reality suffered himself, to be revenged, and he closed his fingers tighter and more rigid till the poor wretch sprang to his feet, and howled with pain!

"Oh! did I hurt you?" he asked with apparent solicitude, as the savage's hand slid from his own with much the appearance of a wet glove. The discomfited Indian made no reply, but retired amid the jeers of his comrades. Seth, without moving a muscle, seated himself deliberately upon the ground, and coolly asked a savage to lend him a pipe. It is known, that when an Indian sees such hardihood and power, as their captor had just evinced, he does not endeavor to conceal his admiration. Thus it was not strange, that Seth's impudent request was complied with. One handed him a well-filled pipe, with a grin in which could be distinctly seen, admiration, exaltation, and anticipated revenge. From the looks of the others, it was plain they anticipated an immense deal of sport. Our present hero continued smoking, lazily watching the volumes of vapor, as they slowly rolled before and around him. His captors sat around him a moment, conversing in their own tongue (every word of which we may remark, was perfectly understood by Seth), when one arose and stepped forward before him.

"White man strong—him pinch well—but me make him cry?"

So saying, he stooped, and removing the captive's cap seized a long tuft of yellow hair which had its root at the temple. A stab in the eye would not have caused an acuter twinge of pain; but, as he jerked it forth by the roots, Seth gave not the slightest indication, save a stronger whiff at the pipe. The savages around did not suppress a murmur of admiration. Seeing no effect from this torture, the tormenter again stooped and caught another tuft that grew low upon the neck. Each single hair felt like the point of a needle thrust into the skin, and as it came forth, the Indians seated around, noticed a livid paleness, like the track of a cloud, quickly flash over their captive's countenance. He looked up in his tormentor's eyes with an indescribable look. For a moment, he fixed a gaze upon him, that savage as he was, caused a strange shiver of dread to run through him.

To say that Seth cared nothing for these inflicted agonies would be absurd. Had the savage dreamed what a whirlwind of hate and revenge he had awakened by them, he would have never attempted what he did. It was only by an almost unaccountable power that Seth controlled the horrible pains of both body and mind, he suffered. He felt as though it was impossible to prevent himself from writhing on the ground in torment, and springing at his persecutor and tearing him from limb to limb. But he had been schooled to Indian indignities, and bore them unflinchingly.

His temple had the appearance of white parchment with innumerable bloody points in it, as the blood commenced oozing from the wound, and his neck seemed as though the skin had been scraped off! His momentary paleness had been caused by the sickening pain and the intensest passion. His look at the savage was to remember him. After the events which have just transpired, they remained seated a moment in silence. At last, one who appeared to be the leader, addressed in an undertone, the Indian whom we have just seen retire from the post of tormentor. Seth, however, caught the words, and had he not, it is not probable he would have successfully undergone the last trying ordeal.

The same savage again stepped forward in the circle before the helpless captive, and removing the cap which had been replaced, clinched the long yellow locks in his left hand, and threw the head backward. Then whipping out his scalping knife, he flashed it a second in the air, and circled its cold edge around his head with the rapidity of lightning. The skin was not pierced, and it was only an artifice. Seth never took his eyes from the Indian during this awful minute.

The tormentor again retired. The savages were satisfied, but Seth was not. He handed his pipe back, replaced his cap, and rising to his feet, surveyed for a few seconds the group around. He then addressed the leader.

"Can the white man now try the red man's courage?"

The voice sounded like another person's. Yet the chief noticed it not, and nodded an assent to the request, while the looks of the others showed the eagerness and interest they felt in these dreadful proceedings.

The savage, who had inflicted all this agony, had seated himself directly beside the chief. Seth stepped to him, and grasping his arm, pressed it moderately. The Indian gave a scornful grunt. Seth then stooped and gently took the tomahawk from his belt. He raised it slowly on high, bent down till his form was like the crouching panther ready to spring. The glittering blade was seen to flash as it circled through the air, and the next instant it crashed clean through the head of the unsuspecting savage!

CHAPTER VIII.
AN UNEXPECTED MEETING.
Wearied and exhausted, Graham crawled forth from the water, and lay down a while to rest himself upon the soft, velvety carpet of grass. Here, overcome by the terrific strain which his system had undergone, he fell into a deep and lasting sleep. When he awoke, the day had far advanced, and the sun was already past the meridian. After fully awakening, and fervently thanking Heaven for his remarkable preservation and escape, he commenced debating with himself upon the best course for him to pursue. He was now alone in the great wilderness, and what step should he next take? Should he endeavor to hunt up his friend Haverland, or should he press on in the pursuit of the object which had led him thus far?

While these questions were yet unanswered, he mechanically cast his eye up the river, and started as he saw a small canoe coming round a bend quite a distance from him. He had just time to see that there were two beings in it, when prudence warned him to make himself invisible. He stepped behind the trunk of a massive king of the forest, and watched with eager interest the approach of the new-comers. The light canoe shot rapidly over the placid surface of the river, and in a few moments was abreast of him. He saw that the two occupants were white men, and he scanned their countenances with deep interest. The stronger of the two was seated in the center of the light vessel, and dipped the ashen blades deep into the water at every stroke. The other, seemingly an elder man, was seated in the stern, and while he controlled the actions of the other, scanned either shore with the experienced eye of the frontiersman. Graham believed, though he knew he had been careful, that his presence was suspected, as the canoe, apparently without any intent of its occupants, sheered off toward the opposite shore. He remained concealed until it was directly abreast of him, when a sudden suspicion flashed over him that one of the men was Haverland, although it was so long since he had seen him that it was impossible to satisfy himself upon that point without a closer view. However, they were white men, and he determined to risk the probabilities of their being friends. In a subdued voice, without coming into view himself, he called to them. He knew he was heard, for the man at the oars halted a second, and glanced furtively toward the shore; but at a slight sign from the other, he again bent to them, and they both continued, as though they suspected no danger.

"Hallo, my friends!" called he, in a louder tone, but still concealing himself. There was no notice, however, taken of him, save he fancied a quicker propulsion of the boat forward. He now stepped boldly forth and called,

"Do not be suspicious; I am a friend."

This brought them to a pause, while the one in the stern spoke.

"We are not satisfied of that; for what business have you here?"

"I might with equal justice put that question to you."

"If you choose to give no answer, we can not wait to bandy words with you. Go ahead, Haverland."

"Hold! is that Alfred Haverland with you?"

"Suppose it is? What is that to you?"

"He is the man whom, above all others, I wish to see. I am Everard Graham; and perhaps he remembers the name."

The woodman now turned toward the shore with a stare of wonder. A minute sufficed.

"It's he, Ned, sure enough."

With these words he turned the canoe toward shore. A few strokes sent it up against the bank, and he sprang out and grasped the hand of his young friend.

"Why, Graham, what in the name of the seven wonders has brought you here? I forgot, you did promise me a visit somewhere about this time, but so many other things have transpired, as to make it slip my mind altogether. And I can assure you, I have had enough to break the heart of any ordinary mortal," he added, in a choking voice.

Explanations were then given; and the wonder, gratitude, and apprehension, that followed Graham's story, may be imagined. Before these were given, Haverland introduced his companion, Ned Haldidge.

"Seth promised to bring Ina back," said he, "but I could not bear to remain idle while he alone was searching for her. This good friend, here, who has had much experience in the border warfare, willingly joined me. I suppose you would like to see the mother; but if you did, you would see a well-nigh broken-hearted one, and I can not bear to meet her until I have learned more of our darling daughter."

"And if them cowardly Mohawks don't rue the day they commenced their infernal work, then Ned Haldidge is mightily mistaken!" exclaimed that individual, warmly.

"I don't know," smiled Graham, "but that with our present number and present feelings, we might make an open attack upon them, especially as we have a friend in the camp."

"No, sir; that'll never do!" replied the hunter, with a shake of the head. "They can never be overcome in that way. We could have brought a dozen men with us who could have blown the cowards to atoms, but 'twouldn't do."

"You then rely wholly upon stratagem, eh?"

"Nothing else will do with them critters."

"And heaven only knows whether that will," remarked Haverland, in a desponding tone.

"Ah! don't give way, Alf, wait till it's time."

"You must pardon my exhibition of weakness," said he, recovering himself. "Though I feel the strength of an army in these limbs of mine, yet I have the heart of a father in this bosom, and I can do any thing for the recovery of my darling daughter. Oh! I can hear her screams yet, as she was torn from us on that night."

Graham and Haldidge remained silent, respecting his deep and moving grief. Soon the father spoke again, and this time his voice and manner were changed.

"But why stand we here idle? Is there nothing for us to do? Are we to remain desponding, when a single effort may save her?"

"That's just what I've been thinking ever since we stopped here," replied Haldidge. "I don't see any use in waiting, especially when there is use in doing something."

"Let us depart, then. You will accompany us, of course, Graham?"

"Certainly; but I should like to inquire your intentions?" asked he, pausing on the bank a moment, as the others seated themselves.

"I should think you would remember we can have but one intention," answered Haverland, in a tone of slight rebuke.

"That is not exactly what I meant. Of course, I knew your ultimate intention, but I wished to inquire what course you intended to pursue."

"Oh, that's it!" replied Haldidge. "I've been considerable among the redskins of this region, and know that they can be soonest reached by going down the river some distance further—several miles below this bend—and taking the land."

"But my experience tells me you are mistaken this time. Ina's captors are now at no great distance, and the shortest course to them, you will find, is in a direct line from here, across the open prairie, the other side the river."

"At any rate, we will cross to the opposite bank; so step in."

"Wait a minute. What does that mean?"

As Graham spoke, he pointed quickly up the river. From the position of the two within the boat, they could discern nothing.

"Jump ashore, quick, and pull the boat out of sight. There's something a-foot, and you musn't be seen," exclaimed Graham excitedly, in an undertone, as he stooped and grasped the prow of the canoe. The men sprang ashore, and in an instant the vessel was hauled up out of sight, while the three made themselves invisible, and from their hiding-places eagerly watched the river.

The object which had arrested the attention of Graham, was a second canoe, which was just making its appearance round the bend above, which had first brought his friends to view. This latter one was of about the same size, and could be seen to hold either three or four persons. The dark-tufted heads of the occupants, rising like statues in the boat, showed unmistakably that they were Indians.

As it came nearer and nearer, Haldidge whispered there was a fourth person in the stern, and she was a female! Haverland and Graham breathed hard, for a wild hope filled the heart of each, but as the canoe came abreast of them, while they could plainly distinguish the features of the three savages, they could not gain a glimpse of the fourth person. She was covered by an Indian shawl, and her head was bowed low upon her bosom, as though in deep and painful thought.

"Let us fire and send these three dogs to eternity," whispered Graham.

Haldidge raised his hand.

"'Twon't do, there may be others about, and if that other one is Ina, it may only be the means of her destruction. Alf, do you think that is her?"

"I can't tell—yes, by heaven, 'tis her! Look! she has moved her shawl. Let us rescue her at once!" exclaimed the father, rising, and about to start.

"Hold!" imperatively and half angrily commanded Haldidge, "you will spoil all by your rashness. Don't you see it is near night? They are now below us, and we can not get them in such a range as to insure us each of them. Wait till it is darker, and we will pursue them. I have a plan which I think can not fail. Just restrain yourself a short time, and I will bring things about in a manner that will surprise them as much as it will you."

Haverland sank down again beside the others. The night was now fast coming on, and in a few minutes the light, birch canoe was shoved noiselessly into the water, and the three made ready for the race of life and death.

CHAPTER IX.
THE CHASE.

The night was even closer at hand than our friends suspected. In the forest, where the withdrawal of the sun was almost simultaneous with darkness, it came without much warning. The gloom was already settling over the water, and Haverland instantly shot the canoe from under the shrubbery out into the stream. There were rowlocks and oars for a second person, and Graham took up a couple and joined his labors with his friend, while Haldidge took the steering oar. As they passed boldly into the channel, the canoe ahead was just disappearing around a bend below.

"Come, this won't do; we musn't let them keep out of our sight," said Haverland, dipping his oars deep into the water.

A heavy darkness was fast settling over the river, and our friends noted another thing. A thick, peculiar fog, or mist, such as is often seen of summer nights, upon a sheet of water, was already beginning to envelop the banks and river. This, as will be evident, while it would allow the pursuers to approach the Indian canoe much closer than otherwise, still gave the latter a much greater chance of eluding them. Haldidge hardly knew whether to be pleased with this or not.

"It may help us in the beginning, boys, but we've got to hold on till it's fairly down on us. If the rascals catch a glimpse of us before, they'll give us the slip as sure as fate. Just lay on your oars a few minutes. We can float down with the current."

"I allow it's the best plan, although I am much in favor of dashing and ending the matter at once," remarked Graham, nervously handling his oars.

"And while I think of it," pursued Haldidge, "I don't see as it would do any hurt to muffle the oars."

Before starting, they had abundantly provided themselves with means for this and, in a few moments a quantity of cloth was forced into the rowlocks, so as to be able to give full sweep to the oars without making enough noise to attract suspicion from the shore, unless an ear was listening more intently than usual.

By this time, too, the thick mist mentioned, had enveloped the river in an impenetrable cloud, and they shot boldly into it. The light vessel flew as swiftly and noiselessly as a bird over the water. Haldidge understood every turn and eddy in the stream, and guided the canoe with unerring certainty around the sharp bends, and by the rocks whose black heads now and then shot backward within a few feet of their side.

In this way a mile was passed when he raised his hand as a signal for them to cease efforts for a moment.

"Listen!" he uttered.

All did so, and faintly, yet distinctly and distantly, they heard the almost inaudible dip of oars, and the click of the rowlocks.

"Is that above or below?" asked Haverland, bending his head and intently listening.

"I think we have passed them sure enough," replied Graham.

The sound certainly appeared to come from above them, and all were constrained to believe that, rowing as swiftly and powerfully as they did, they must have swept by them in the darkness without suspecting their proximity.

"Can it be possible?" questioned Haldidge, wonderingly and doubtingly.

But such was the character of the river-banks at this point, that all had been deceived in listening to the sounds, and the Indians were all the time leaving them far behind. It was not until they heard unmistakably the sounds receding in the distance, that they became conscious of the true state of matters. At that moment, as they were dying out, they all heard them plainly enough far below.

"We might have known it," said Haldidge in vexation. "You've got to lay to it, to catch them now."

"But is there not danger of running afoul of them?"

"Not if we are careful. I think they will run into shore soon, and if so, it will be the eastern bank. I will hug that closely, and keep my ears open."

The two now bent to their oars with redoubled powers. They dipped the ashen blades deeply, and pulled until they bent dangerously, while the water parted in foam at its rushing prow, and spread away in a foamy pyramid behind.

The effect of this was soon apparent. The rattle of the oars ahead grew plainer and plainer at each stroke, and it was evident that they were gaining finely. Haverland's arm was thrilled with tenfold power, as he felt that he was rushing to the rescue of his only darling child, and he only wished he might have the chance to spring upon her abductors and rend them limb from limb. Graham's heart beat faster as he reflected that, perhaps, in a few moments, he should be face to face with her who had hovered about his pillow in all his visions for many a night.

Haldidge sat perfectly cool and possessed. He had formed his plan, and imparted it to the others; it was to pursue the canoe noiselessly until they were almost upon it, when the instant they were near enough to distinguish forms, they would fire upon the Indians, and dash ahead and capture Ina at all hazards.

This Haldidge, who has been introduced to notice in this chapter, was a middle-aged man, who ten years before had emigrated from the settlements along the Hudson, with a company which had formed the settlement from which he started, and where we saw Haverland and his wife and sister safely domiciled. He was a married man, and his cabin happened to be upon the outskirts of the village. He joined and led the whites in several forays against the savages, when the latter became too troublesome; and, in this way he at last became a prominent object for the Indian's hatred. His residence became known to them, and one dark, stormy night a half-dozen made a descent upon it. By the merest chance, Haldidge was in the village at that time, and thus escaped their malignant revenge. Being disappointed of their principal prey, they cowardly vented their hatred upon his defenseless wife and child. When the father returned, he found them both tomahawked, side by side, and weltering in each other's blood. So silently had this onslaught been made that not a neighbor suspected any thing wrong, and were horror-struck to find that such deadly peril had been so near their own door. Haldidge took a fearful vengeance upon the destroyers of his happiness. He succeeded, a couple of years afterward, in discovering them, and, before six months were over, shot them all! As may be supposed, his natural aversion to the race, was intensified by this tragical occurrence, and had become so distinguished, that his name was as a terror to the savages in that section. This will account for his readiness in accompanying Haverland upon his perilous expedition.

As was said, our friends were rapidly gaining upon the Indian canoe. At the rate at which they were going, they would be up to them in the course of a half hour. They were so close to the shore, as to see the dark line of the shrubbery along the bank, and several times an overhanging limb brushed over their heads. Suddenly Haldidge raised his hand again. All ceased rowing and listened. To their consternation not the slightest sound was heard. Graham leaned over, and placed his ear almost to the water, but detected nothing but the soft ripple of the stream against the roots and dipping branches along the shore.

"Can it be?" he asked, with a painful whisper, as he raised his head, "that we have been heard?"

"I do not think so," replied Haldidge, apparently in as much doubt as the rest.

"Then they have run into shore, and departed."

"I fear that has been done."

"But we have kept so close to the shore, would we not have seen or heard the boat?"

41

"Provided they had landed alone. They may have run in this very minute, and may not be more than a few yards off."

"If so, we must hear them yet, and it won't do to slide down upon them in the manner we are now going or we shall find ourselves in the same fix we expected to get them in."

"Very true, and a good suggestion," remarked Haldidge; and as he did so, he reached up and caught an overhanging limb, and held the canoe still.

"Now, boys, if you've got ears——"

"Sh—! Look there!" interrupted Haverland in an excited whisper.

Each turned his head, and saw what appeared to be a common lighted candle floating upon the surface of the stream. It was a small point of light, which at intervals glowed with a fuller redness, and which for the time completely confounded our friends. On it came as noiselessly as death, gliding forward with such a smooth, regular motion as to show that it was certainly borne by the current.

"What in the name of——"

"Stop!" cried Haldidge; "that's the canoe we're after! It's the light of one of their pipes we see. Are your guns ready?"

"Yes," replied the two, just loud enough for him to hear.

"Make right toward it, then, and fire the instant you see your mark. Now!"

At the same instant he released his hold upon the limb, and the two threw all their force on their oars. The canoe bounded like a ball directly ahead, and seemed about to cut the other in twain. A minute after, the shadowy outlines of three forms could be dimly seen, and the avenging rifles were already raised, when the beacon-light was suddenly extinguished, and the Indian canoe vanished as if by magic.

"It's one of their tricks!" excitedly exclaimed Haldidge. "Dash ahead! Curse them; they can't be far off."

The two dropped their rifles, and again seized the oars, and Haldidge sheered it abruptly up stream, for he fancied they had turned in that direction. He bent his head forward, expecting each moment to see the forms of their enemies loom up to view in the mist, but he was mistaken; no savages greeted his anxious vision. He guided his boat in every direction—across the stream—

up and down, but all to no purpose. They had surely lost their prey this time. The Indians had undoubtedly heard the pursuers—had muffled their own oars, and so proceeded as silently as their pursuers.

"Hold a minute!" commanded Haldidge.

As they rested, they listened deeply and intently.

"Do you hear any thing?" he asked, leaning breathlessly forward. "There! listen again."

They could distinguish the ripple of water, growing fainter and fainter, each minute.

"They are below us again, and now for a trial of speed."

The two needed no more incentives, and for a time the canoe skimmed over the water with astonishing speed. The moon was now up, and there were patches in the stream, where the wind had blown away the fog, and being exposed to the light, were as clear as midday. Now and then they crossed such spots, sometimes but a few feet wide, and at others, several rods. At these times the shore on either hand were perfectly outlined, and they glided over them with a sort of instinctive terror, as they felt how easily an enemy might be concealed.

In crossing one of these, broader than usual, a glimpse of the Indian canoe showed itself, just disappearing upon the opposite side. They were not more than a hundred yards apart, and they bounded toward it with great rapidity. The patches of light became more frequent, and the fog was evidently disappearing. Quite a breeze had arisen, which was fast sweeping it away. Haldidge kept close into the eastern shore, feeling sure that their enemies would land upon this side.

Suddenly the whole mist lifted from the surface of the water in a volume, and rolled off into the woods. The bright moon was reflected a long distance, and the pursuers gazed searchingly about, fully expecting to see their enemies not a dozen rods away. But they were again doomed to disappointment. Not a ripple disturbed the waters, except their own canoe. The moon was directly overhead, so that there was not a shadow cast along the banks, sufficient to conceal the slightest object. The Indians had evidently landed, and were far distant in the forest.

"It is no use," remarked Haverland, gloomily, "they are gone, and we might as well be—too."

"It is a sore disappointment," added Graham.

"And as much so to me as to either of you," said Haldidge. "I have an old score against the infernal wretches that will take many years to wipe out. I hoped to do something toward it to-night, but have been prevented. There is no use of hoping more at this time; they have eluded us, that is self-evident, and we must try some other means. No doubt you are wearied of body as well as of mind, and don't fancy particularly this remaining out in the river here, a shot for any one who might possess the will; so let us go into shore, have a rest, and talk over things." Dispiritedly and gloomily the two ran the canoe to the bank and landed.

CHAPTER X.
A COUPLE OF INDIAN CAPTIVES.

So sudden, so unexpected, so astounding was the crash of Seth's tomahawk through the head of the doomed savage, that, for a moment after, not an Indian moved or spoke. The head was nearly cleft in twain (for an arm fired by consuming passion had driven it), and the brains were spattered over numbers of those seated around. Seth himself stood a second, as if to satisfy himself that the work was complete, when he turned, walked to his seat, sat down, coolly folded his arms, and commenced whistling!

A second after, nearly every savage drew a deep breath, as if a load had been removed from his heart; then each looked at his neighbor, and in the scowling, ridged brows, the glittering eyes, the distorted visages, the strained breathing through the set teeth, could be read the fearful intention. Every face but that of the chieftain's, was livid with fury. He alone sat perfectly unagitated. Three Indians arose, and, grasping their knives, stood before him waiting for the expected words.

"Touch him not," said he, with a shake of the head; "him, no right here."

As the chief spoke, he tapped his forehead significantly with his finger, meaning that the prisoner was demented. The others believed the same, still it was hard to quell the pent-up fire which was scorching their breasts. But his word was law inviolate, and without a murmur, they seated themselves upon the ground again.

Seth, although his eye appeared vacant and unmeaning, had noted all these movements with the keenness of the eagle. He knew that a word or sign from the chief would be sufficient to hack him into a thousand pieces. When he stood before his inhuman tormentor, with the keen tomahawk in his hand, the certainty of instant death or prolonged torture would not have prevented him taking the savage vengeance he did. Now that it was over, he was himself again. His natural feelings came back, and with it the natural desire for life. The words

44

of the chief convinced him that he was regarded as either insane or idiotic, and consequently as not deserving death. Still, although saved for the present, he ever stood in imminent peril. The fallen savage had living friends, who would seize the first opportunity to avenge his death. At any rate, let matters stand as they might, Seth felt that he was in hot quarters, and the safest course was to get out of them as soon as possible.

It was perhaps ten minutes after the horrid deed, that the savages commenced bestirring themselves. Several arose and carried their comrade to one side, while the others commenced preparations for taking up the day's march. At this moment, the runners who had pursued Graham to the water's edge, returned, and the tragical occurrence was soon made known to them. A perfect battery of deadly gleaming eyes was opened upon Seth, but he stood it unflinchingly. The Indians would have relished well the idea of venting their baffled vengeance upon the helpless captive in their hands; but the commanding presence of their chief restrained the slightest demonstration, and they contented themselves with meaning looks.

One thing did not escape Seth's notice from the first, and it was an occasion of wonder and speculation to him. Nothing could be seen of Ina. In fact, the appearance of things was such as to lead one to believe that the savages knew nothing of her. Could it be that he and Graham had been mistaken in the party? Could some other tribe have made off with her? Or, had they separated, and taken her in an other direction? As he ruminated upon these questions, he became convinced that the last suggested the certain answer. They could not have mistaken the party, as they had never lost sight of the trail since taking it; and, moreover, he had noticed several slight occurrences, since his advent among them, that satisfied him, beyond a doubt, of the identity of the party with the one which had descended upon the home of the woodman. From the caution which the aggressors evidenced in their flight, together with the haste in which it had been conducted; it was plain they had some fears of pursuit; and to guard their treasure, a number had left them at a favorable point, intending to join the main body where pursuit was not to be expected, or where the pursuers had been sufficiently misled to warrant it. As he reflected, Seth was satisfied that this was the only and the true explanation of her non-appearance at this time.

The preparations were soon completed, and the Indians commenced moving forward. If Seth had entertained any doubts of their intentions relating to him, they were soon dispelled by his experience. It was not at all likely that he would be reserved as a prisoner, unless they intended to put him to some use. Accordingly, he found himself loaded down with an enormous burden, consisting mostly of food, in the shape of deer's meat, which the savages had brought with them. They buried their fallen comrade, without the ceremony and mourning which might be expected. The North American Indian rarely gives way to his emotions, except upon such occasions as the burial of one of their number, a "war dance," or something similar, when the whole nest of devilish passions is allowed free vent. They indulged in no such ceremonies—if ceremonies they may be called—at this time. A comparatively shallow grave was dug, and into this the fallen one was placed in an upright position, his face turned toward the east. His rifle, knives, and all his clothing were buried with him.

The day was a suffocating one in August, and Seth's sufferings were truly great. He was naturally lithe, wiry, and capable of enduring prolonged exertion; but, unfortunately for him, the savages had become aware of this and had loaded him accordingly. Most of the journey was through the forest, where the arching tree-tops, shut out the withering rays of the sun. Had they encountered any such open plains, as the one passed over, near their encampment, Seth would have never lived to survive it. As it was, his load nearly made him insensible to pain. A consuming thirst was ever tormenting him, although he found abundant means to slake it in the numberless rills which gurgled through the wilderness.

"How Yankee like it?" grinned a savage, by his side, stooping and peering fiendishly into his face.

"First rate; goes nice. Say, you, s'posen you try it?"

"Ugh! walk faster," and a whack accompanied the word.

"Now, I cac'late I'm going to walk just about as fast as I darned please, and if you ain't a mind to wait, you can heave ahead. Fact, by gracious."

And Seth did not increase his steps in the least. Toward noon, he found he should be obliged to have a short rest or give out entirely. He knew it would be useless to ask, and consequently he determined to take it without asking. So, unloosing the cords which bound the pack to his back, he let it fall to the ground, and, seating himself upon it, again went to whistling!

"Go faster, Yankee—you no keep up," exclaimed one, giving him a stunning blow.

"See here, you, p'raps you don't know who it mought be you insulted in that way. I'm Seth Jones, from New Hampshire, and consequently you'll be keerful of tetching me."

The savage addressed, was upon the point of striking him insolently to the earth, when the chieftain interfered.

"No touch pale face—him tired—rest a little."

Some unaccountable whim had possessed the savage, as this mercy was entirely unexpected by Seth, and he knew not how to account for it, unless it might be he was reserving him for some horrible torture.

The resting spell was but a breathing moment, however, and just as Seth had begun to really enjoy it, the chieftain gave orders for the replacement of the load. Seth felt disposed to tamper awhile, for the sake of prolonging his enjoyment, but, on second thought, concluded it the better plan not to cross the chief who had been so lenient to him thus far. So, with a considerable number of original remarks, and much disputation about the placing of the burden, he shouldered it at last and trudged forward.

Seth was right in his conjectures about Ina. Toward the latter part of the day, the three Indians who had been pursued by our other friends, rejoined the main party, bearing her with them. She noticed her companion in captivity at once, but no communication passed between them. A look of melancholy relief escaped her as she became assured that her parents were still safe, and that only she and her new friend were left to the sufferings and horrors of captivity. But there was enough in this to damp even such a young and hopeful spirit as was hers. Not death alone, but a fate from the sensuous captors, far worse than death itself, was to be apprehended. In the future, there was but one Hand that could sustain and safely deliver them, and to that One she looked for deliverance.

CHAPTER XI.
STILL IN PURSUIT.
"It seems the devil himself is helping them imps!" remarked Haldidge as they landed.

"But I trust Heaven is aiding us," added Haverland.

"Heaven will if we help ourselves, and now as I'm in this scrape I'm bound to see the end. Look for trail."

"It's poor work I'm thinking we'll make, groping in this moonlight," said Graham.

"While there's life there's hope. Scatter 'long the bank, and search every foot of land. I'll run up stream a ways as I've an idea they landed not fur off."

The hunter disappeared with these words, and Graham and Haverland, commenced their work in an opposite direction. The branches overhanging the water were carefully lifted up, and the muddy shore examined; the suspicious bending or parting of the undergrowth was followed by the minutest scrutiny, and although the heavy darkness was against them, yet it would have required a most guarded trail to have escaped their vision. But their efforts were useless; no trail was detected; and convinced that the savages must have landed upon the opposite side, they turned to retrace their steps. As they did so, a low whistle from the hunter reached their ears.

"What does that mean?" asked Graham.

"He has discovered something. Let us hasten."

"What is it, Haldidge?" asked Haverland as they reached the hunter.

"Here's their tracks as sure as I'm a sinner, and it's my private opine they ain't fur off neither."

"Shall we wait until daylight before we undertake to follow it?"

"I am much afraid we shall have to, as there may be signs which we might miss in this darkness. Day can't be far off."

"Several hours yet."

"Well, we will make ourselves comfortable until then."

With these words the trio seated themselves upon the earth, and kept up a low conversation until morning. As soon as the faint light appeared, they detected the Indian canoe a short distance up the bank, secreted beneath a heavy, overhanging mass of undergrowth. As it was during the summer season, their pursuit was continued at an early hour, so the savages could have had but a few hours start at the most. With Ina they could not proceed very rapidly, and our friends were sanguine of overtaking them ere the day closed.

The only apprehension the pursuers felt, was that the three savages, fully conscious now that their enemies were upon their trail, might hasten to rejoin the main body, and thus cut off all hope. They could not be many miles apart, and must have made some preparation for this contingency.

The trail to the hunter's eye was distinct and easily followed. He took the lead, striding rapidly forward, while Haverland and Graham were continually on

48

the look-out for danger. Haverland was somewhat fearful that the savages, finding they could not avoid being overtaken, would halt and form an ambush into which the hunter would blindly lead them. The latter, however, although he appeared culpably rash and heedless, understood Indian tactics better; he knew no halt would be made until the savages were compelled to do so.

"Ah!—see here!" exclaimed Haldidge, suddenly pausing.

"What's the trouble?" queried Graham, stepping hastily forward with Haverland.

"Their camping ground, that is all."

Before them were more visible signs of the trail than they had yet witnessed. A heap of ashes were upon the ground; and, as Haverland kicked them apart, he discovered the embers still red and glowing. Sticks were broken and scattered around, and all the varied evidences of an Indian camp were to be seen.

"How long ago was this place vacated?" asked Graham.

"Not three hours."

"We must be close upon them."

"Rather, yes."

"Let us hasten forward then."

"You see by these coals that they didn't start until daylight; and as that gal of yourn, Haverland, can't travel very fast, of course they've had to take their time."

"Very true; although disappointment has attended us thus far, I begin to feel a little of my natural hope return. I trust that this opportunity will not escape us."

"Ah! more signs yet," exclaimed Graham, who had been examining the ground for several yards around.

"What now?"

"That's a piece of her dress is it not?"

49

And he held up small, fluttering rag in his hands. The father eagerly took it, and examined it.

"Yes; that is Ina's; I hope no violence has placed it in our hands," and several involuntary tears coursed down his cheek at the allusion.

"I'm thinking she left it there on purpose to guide us," remarked Graham.

"Shouldn't wonder at all," added Haldidge.

"She must have seen us, of course, and has done all she could to guide us."

"Very probable; but it strikes me rather forcibly that we are gaining nothing in particular by remaining here. Remember the savages are going all the time."

Thus admonished, the three set rapidly forward again, the hunter taking the lead as before. The pursuit was kept up without halting until near noon. Conscious that they were rapidly gaining upon the fugitives, it was necessary to proceed with the extremest caution. The breaking of a twig, the falling of a leaf, startled and arrested their steps, and not a word was exchanged except in the most careful whisper. Haldidge was some dozen yards in advance, and the eyes of his companions were upon him, when they saw him suddenly pause and raise his hand as a signal for them to halt. They did so, and stooping downward, he commenced examining the leaves before him. A moment sufficed. He turned and motioned his two companions forward.

"Just as I feared," he moodily exclaimed in a half whisper.

"What's the matter?" asked Haverland anxiously.

"The two trails join here," he answered.

"Are you not mistaken?" asked Haverland, knowing that he was not, and yet catching at the faintest hope held out to him.

"No, sir; there's no mistake. Instead of three Indians, we've got over forty to follow up now."

"Shall we do it?"

"Shall we do it? of course we shall; it's the only chance of ever getting a sight of Ina again."

"I know so, and yet the hope is so faint; they must know we are in pursuit, and what can we do against ten times our number?"

"No telling yet; come, strike ahead again."

With these words, the hunter turned and plunged deeper into the forest. Graham and Haverland silently followed, and, in a few moments, the three were proceeding as carefully and silently as before through the dense wood.

As yet our friends had partaken of nothing, and began to experience the pangs of hunger; but, of course, in the present instance these were disregarded. Somewhere near the middle of the afternoon, they came upon another spot where the savages had halted. Here, if Haverland and Graham had any lingering doubts of what the hunter had said, they were soon removed. It was plain that a large Indian party had halted upon this spot but a few hours before, and it was equally evident that they had taken no pains to conceal the traces they had made. If they had any suspicions of pursuit, they had no apprehensions of the consequences, as they were well aware of the disparity between the two forces, and scorned the whites.

This was gratifying on the other hand to the hunter. He knew well enough that as matters stood at present, he could hope for nothing except through his own cunning and stratagem; and, for this reason, it was very probable the Indians were satisfied no attempt would be made. They did not take into consideration the fact that there was an enemy in their camp.

Considerable remains of the meal were discovered, and served to satisfy the wants of our friends for the present. The early time in the afternoon showed them that thus far they had gained quite rapidly upon the savages. It was the earnest wish of the three that they should come up to the Indian party by nightfall; but this expectation was doomed to a sudden disappointment; for in a few hours they reached a point where the trail divided again.

This was unaccountable even to the hunter, and for a few moments our friends stood perfectly nonplussed. They had not looked for this, and had not the slightest reason of it.

"This beats all creation!" remarked Haldidge, as he again examined the trail.

"Depend upon it there is something meant in this," observed Haverland with an air of deep concern.

"It is some stratagem of the imps which we must understand before going further."

"They must entertain different ideas of us from what we thought. You may safely believe that this is some plan to mislead us, and if there is ever a time when our wits shall be demanded it has now come."

During this fragmentary conversation, the hunter was minutely examining the trail. Graham and Haverland watched him a few seconds in silence, when the latter asked:

"Do you make any thing of it?"

"Nothing more. The trail divides here; the main body proceeds onward in a direct line, while the minor trail leads off to the west. The division must have been very unequal, for as near as I can judge the smaller party does not number over three or four at the most. No efforts have been made to conceal their traces, and there is either a deep laid scheme afloat, or they don't care a fig for us."

"Very probably both," remarked Graham. "They care enough for us to take good care to remain out of our reach, when they do not possess advantages over us, and have already shown their skill in not only laying but in executing schemes."

"If we could only give that Seth Jones an inkling of our whereabouts and intentions, I should feel pretty sanguine again," said Haverland.

"Very likely if that Jones could give us an inkling of his whereabouts and experiences, you would lose a little of that expectation," rejoined the hunter with a meaning emphasis and look.

"But this is a waste of time and words," said Graham, "let us lay our heads together and decide at once what is to be done. As for me, I'm in favor of following the smaller party."

"What give you that idea?" asked Haverland.

"I confess that I cannot give much reason for the notion, but somehow or other it has struck me that Ina is with the smaller party."

"Hardly probable," returned Haverland.

"It don't seem so, I allow," remarked the hunter; "but queerly enough the same notion has got into my head."

"Of course you can then give some reason."

"I can give what appears to have a show of reason to me. I have been doing a big amount of thinking for the last few minutes, and have almost reached a conclusion. I believe that the gal is with the smaller party, and it is the wish of the savages that we shall follow the main body. We will thus be drawn into ambush, and all further trouble from us will be removed."

"It seems hardly probable that the savages would run such a risk of losing their captive when there is no occasion for it," remarked Haverland.

"It don't seem probable, but it ain't the first thing they've done (providing of course they've done it), that would make you open your eyes. I believe these Mohawks are certain we won't suspect they've let the gal go off with two or three of their number when there were enough to watch her and keep her out the hands of a dozen such as we are. Feeling certain of this, I say they have let her go; and being sure also that we'll tramp on after them, they have made arrangements some distance away from here to dispose of us."

"Sound reasoning, I admit, but here's something to offer upon the other side," said Graham producing another fluttering rag from a bush.

"How is that upon the other side of the question?" queried the hunter.

"If you will notice the bush from which I took this, you will see it is upon the trail of the larger party, and consequently Ina must have been with that party to have left it there."

"Just show me the exact twig from which you took it," quietly asked Haldidge. Graham led the way a few yards off and showed him the spot. The hunter stooped and carefully examined the bush.

"I'm now satisfied," said he, "that I was right. That rag was left there by a savage for the express purpose of misleading us. We must seek Ina in another direction."

"Haldidge," said Haverland earnestly, "I place great reliance upon your skill and judgment, but it strikes me at this moment that you are acting capriciously against reason."

"There's but one way to decide it; will you agree to it?" asked the hunter smilingly. The other two expressed their willingness, and he produced his hunting knife. For fear that some of our readers may be apprehensive of the use to which he intended putting it, we will describe his modus operandi at once. Stepping back a pace or two, the hunter took the point of his knife between his thumb and fore finger, and flung it over his head. As it fell to the earth again, the point was turned directly toward the trail of the lesser party.

"Just what I thought," remarked the hunter with another quiet smile. The mooted question was now settled to the satisfaction of all, and our three friends turned unhesitatingly to the westward upon the trail of the smaller party.

How much sometimes hangs upon the slightest thread! How small is the point upon which great events often turn! The simple fact of the direction in which the blade of the hunting knife remained when it fell, decided the fate of every character in this life drama. Had it pointed to the northward, an hour later the three would have walked into an ambush intended for them, and every one would have been massacred. The hunter was right. Ina Haverland had gone with the smaller party.

CHAPTER XII.
PENCILINGS BY THE WAY.
We have said the hunter was right. By the accidental turning of the hunting knife, he had not only been saved his life, but his efforts had been turned in the right direction.

It must be confessed that Haverland himself had some misgivings about the course which they were taking. He could not believe that the savages were short-sighted enough to place a captive which was secure in their possession, into the hands of one or two of their number, when they were conscious they were pursued. But the decision of the hunting knife could not be appealed from, and in a moody silence he followed in the footsteps of the hunter.

It was now getting far along in the afternoon, and the pursued savages could be at no great distance. Their trail was plain, as no efforts had been made to conceal it; but, although Haldidge strove his utmost to detect signs of Ina's delicate moccasin, he failed entirely; and was compelled, in spite of the assurance which he manifested at the start, to take some misgivings to himself.

The hunter, notwithstanding the consummate cunning and skill he had shown thus far in tracing up the savages, had made one sad mistake. He had been misled altogether in the number of the smaller party. Instead of three or four Indians, there were six; and, as their trails became visible at intervals, he began to think he had undertaken a more difficult matter than he anticipated. Still, it was no time for halting or faltering, and he strode resolutely forward.

"Ah—some more signs," exclaimed he, stopping suddenly.

"What are they?" queried his companions eagerly.

"Just notice this bush, if you please, and tell me what you make of it."

The two friends did so, and saw that one of the branches of some sprouts of chestnut, growing round a stump, had been broken short off, and lay pointing toward the trail.

"I make it favorable. Ina has done this to guide us," said Haverland.

"My opinion exactly," added Graham.

"You are mistaken about one thing. Ina did not do it."

"Did not do it?" exclaimed the others; "and who did then?"

"That's the question. I'm of the opinion that that white man you have told me about, has done it."

"But it can not be that he is with them, too."

"Surely it is impossible that the Indians would allow both of their captives to be in charge of two or three of their number at the same time."

"As for two or three, there are six painted Mohawks ahead of us for that matter. I haven't detected the trail of the gal yet, but have discovered several times pretty convincing evidence that a white man is among them. If you will look at that stick again, you will see that it is not likely your gal broke it. In the first place I don't believe she is able; for notice how thick it is; and, if she could have done it, it would have taken so much time, that she would have been prevented."

"Very probably Seth is among them, although it is singular to say the least. Some unaccountable whim has taken possession of the Indians."

"But you say you discern nothing of Ina's trail?" asked Graham.

"Not as yet."

"Do you think she is among them?"

"I do."

"Where is her trail then?"

"Somewhere on the ground, I suppose."

"Well, why have we not seen it, then?"

"I suppose, because it has escaped our eyes."

"A good explanation," smiled Graham, "but if we have failed altogether thus far to detect it, is it probable that she is among them?"

"I think so. You must remember that these half dozen Mohawks are walking promiscuously and not in Indian file, as is generally their custom. It is very probable that the gal is in front, and what tracks her little moccasins might make would be entirely covered up with the big feet of the Ingins."

"I hope you are not mistaken," remarked Haverland, in such a tone as to show that he still had his lingering doubts.

"That matter can not be decided until we get a peep of the dusky cowards, and the only course is for us to push ahead."

"It strikes me that they can be at no great distance, and if we are going to come upon their camp-fire to-night, we have got to do it pretty soon."

"Come on, then."

With this, the hunter again strode forward, but with more stealth and caution than before. He saw in the different signs around them unmistakable proof that the Indians were at no great distance.

Just as the sun was setting, the triumvirate reached a small stream which dashed and foamed directly across the trail. They halted a moment to slake their thirst, and the hunter arose and moved forward again. But Graham made it a point to search at every halting place for guiding signs, and he called out to his companions to wait a moment.

"Time is too precious," replied he, "and you won't find any thing here."

"Won't find any thing here, eh? Just come and look at this."

The hunter stepped back over the stones in the brook, and with Haverland approached Graham. The latter pointed to a broad, flat stone at his feet. Upon it was scratched, with some softer stone, the following words:—

"Hurry forward. There are six Indians, and they have got Ina with them. They don't suspect you are following them, and are hurrying up for the village. I think we will camp two or three miles from here. Make the noise of the whipporwil when you want to do the business, and I will understand.

Yours, respectfully,
Seth Jones."

"If I warn't afraid the imps would hear it, I would vote three cheers for that Jones," exclaimed Haldidge, "he's a trump whoever he is."

"You may depend upon that," added Graham, "for what little I saw of him was sufficient to show me that."

"Let me see," repeated the hunter, again reading the writing upon the stone, "he says they will encamp two or three miles from here. The sun has now set, but we shall have light for over an hour yet, sufficient to guide us. It's best for us to be moving forward, as there is no time to spare."

"It beats my time how that Jones got into this crowd," said Graham, half to himself, as the three again moved forward.

"He's there, we know, and that is enough for the present; when we have the time to spare, we may speculate upon the matter. All ready."

"Yes,—but a moment. Haldidge, let us have some arrangement about the manner in which we are going to travel. Double caution is now necessary."

"I will keep my eyes upon the trail, as I have done all along, and see that we don't walk into a hornet's nest, with our eyes shut. You can help keep a look-out, while you, Graham, who have been so lucky thus far in stumbling upon what neither of us saw, will watch for more signs. Just as like as not, that Jones has been clever enough to give us some more good directions."

Each understanding his duty, now prepared to fulfil it. The progress was necessarily slow, from the extreme caution exercised.

The hunter had proceeded but a short distance, when he noticed his shadow was cast upon the ground; and, looking up, saw to his regret, that the full moon was in the heavens. This was unfortunate for them; for, although it discovered the trail with as much certainty as in the day, and thus assisted them in the pursuit; yet the chances of their approach being made known to the Indians, was almost certain.

"Hist!" suddenly called Graham, in a whisper.

"What's up now?" asked the hunter, turning stealthily around.

"Some more writing from Seth."

Haverland and Haldidge approached. Graham was stooping beside a flat stone, endeavoring to decipher some character upon it. The light of the moon, although quite strong, was hardly sufficient. By dint of patience and perseverance, they succeeded in reading the following:

"Be VERY careful. The imps begin to suspect; they have seen me making signs, and are suspicious. They keep a close watch on the gal. Remember the signal, when you come up with us. Yours, in haste, but nevertheless with great respect.

Seth Jones, Esq."

It was now evident that they were in close proximity to the savages. After a moment's hurried debate, it was decided that Haldidge should walk at a greater distance ahead than heretofore, and communicate instantly with his companions, upon discovering the camp.

Slowly, silently, and cautiously the three moved forward. A half-hour later, Graham touched the shoulder of Haverland, and pointing meaningly ahead. A red reflection was seen in the branches overhead; and, as they stood in silence, the glimmer of a light was seen through the trees. The next instant, the hunter stood beside them.

"We've come on to them at last;" he whispered, "see that your priming is all right, and make up your mind for hot work."

They had already done this, and were anxious for the contest to be decided. Their hearts beat high, as they realized how near the deadly conflict was, and even the hunter's breath was short and hurried. But there was no faltering or wavering, and they moved stealthily forward.

CHAPTER XIII.
SOME EXPLANATIONS.

The village of the Mohawks was at a considerable distance from the spot where had once stood the home of the woodman—and encumbered as they were with plunder, their progress was necessarily slow; besides, knowing full well that pursuit would be useless upon the part of the whites, there was no occasion to hasten their steps. When, however, Seth Jones' unceremonious entrance among them, together with the escape of his new companion, and the subsequent report of the smaller party with Ina, was made known, the old chief began to have some misgiving about his fancied security. It occurred to him that there might be a large party of whites upon the trail, and in such a case, his greatest skill was required to retain the captives. And here was the trouble. If he was pursued—and upon that point there could be no doubt—his progress must be hastened. His pursuers would follow with the swiftness of vengeance. With the plunder in their possession, the thing was impossible, and he saw, at length, that stratagem must be resorted to.

He selected six of his bravest and fleetest warriors—two of whom had been Graham's most troublesome enemies in his fearful chase—and placed Ina in their charge, with instructions to make all haste to the Indian village. Before starting, it occurred to him that the best plan would be to send the white man also with them. Were he to remain with the larger party in case of attack, his presence, he had reason to fear, would be their own destruction, while six savages surely armed and ever vigilant, could surely guard an unarmed idiot and a woman.

The chief as stated, was well satisfied that he was pursued. Hence, if he could throw his pursuers off the scent, their discomfiture would be certain. He believed this could be done. How well he succeeded, has already been shown. The six savages with their charge parted from the larger company, and struck off rapidly in a direction diverging to the north. Their trail was so concealed as to give the impression that there were but three of them, and this deception we have seen misled the hunter. A piece of Ina's dress was purposely lodged upon a bush, in the rear of the larger party; and promiscuously and hopefully, the chief leisurely continued his way with his dusky followers.

After the parties had parted company, the smaller one hastened rapidly forward. Ina, in charge of a stalwart, athletic Indian was kept to the front, the more effectually to conceal her trail, while Seth kept his position near the centre of the file. He was allowed the free use of his hands, though, as has been remarked, he was deprived of his weapons. As they journeyed hastily forward, he made it a point to enlighten them as much as possible by his conversation, and certainly original remarks.

"If you have no objection, I wouldn't mind knowing your idea in thus leaving the other Injins, eh?" he remarked, quizzically of the savage in front. No reply being given, he continued:

"I s'pose you're thinking about that house you burnt down, and feeling bad—Oh, you ain't, eh?" suddenly remarked Seth, as the Indian glared fiercely at him.

"It was a bad trick, I allow," he continued, "enough to make a feller mad, I swow. That house, I shouldn't wonder now, took that Haverland a week to finish; 'twas an ugly piece of business—yes, sir."

At intervals, the savages exchanged a word with each other, and once or twice, one of them took the back trail, evidently to ascertain whether they had any pursuers. Finding they had not, they slackened their speed somewhat, as Ina had given signs of fatigue, and they believed there was really no occasion for hastening. But the weariness which the fair captive had endured, so increased, that long before the sun had reached its meridian, they halted for a half-hour's rest. This was at the crossing of a small, sparkling stream. As the sun was now quite hot, and the atmosphere thick and heavy, the rest in the cool shadows of the trees was doubly refreshing. Ina seated herself upon the cool moist earth, her captors preserving, singularly enough, a far more vigilant watch over her than over Seth Jones; but, for that matter, the latter was allowed no very special freedom. A couple of Indians again took the back-trail for prudent reasons, but met with nothing to excite their apprehensions.

In the mean time, Seth continued tumbling over the ground, occasionally giving vent to snatches of song, and now and then a sage remark. Without being noticed, he picked a small chalky pebble from the margin of the brook, and working his way to a large flat stone, executed, with many flourishes, the writing to which we referred in a preceding chapter. Although cleverly done, this latter act did not escape the eyes of the suspicious savages. One immediately arose, and walking to him, pointed down and gruffly asked:

"What, that?"

"Read it fur yourself," replied Seth innocently.

"What, that?" repeated the savage, menacingly.

"A little flourishing I was executing, jist to pass away time."

"Ugh!" grunted the Indian, and dipping his big foot in the brook, he irreverently swept it across the stone, completely wiping out Seth's beautiful chirography.

"Much obliged," said the latter, "saved me the trouble. I can write on it again when it gits dry."

But no opportunity was given, as a moment after the scouts returned, and the line of march was taken up. But Seth well knew he had accomplished all that could be desired. He had taken particular pains that the pebble should be flinty enough to scratch into the soft stone every word that he wrote. Consequently, the party had not been gone a half-hour, when every letter came but as clear and distinct as before, despite the wet daub the indignant savage had given it.

Their progress for a time was quite rapid. Seth, somehow or other, was constantly pitching out of file, breaking down the twigs along the way, stumbling against the stones which were not in the way, and, in spite of the menaces and occasional blows of his captors, making the trail unnecessarily distinct and plain.

At noon, another halt was made, and all partook of some food. Ina was sick at heart, and ate but a mouthful. An apprehension of her dreadful position came over her, and her soul reeled as she began picturing what was yet to come. Seth quarreled with two of his captors, because, he affirmed, they took more than their share of the dinner; and, take it all in all, affairs were getting into as interesting a state as one could well conceive.

The meal finished, they again set forward. From the whispered consultation of the savages, as well as the words which reached Seth's ears, and their utter disregard of Ina's painful fatigue, he began to believe that the Indians suspected that their stratagem had not misled their pursuers, and were apprehensive of pursuit. Finally, Seth became satisfied that such was the case, and when they halted toward the middle of the afternoon, he again gave vent to his thoughts upon a friendly stone which offered itself, and this, again, received a fierce wipe from the foot of the same savage, and the words again came out to view, and accomplished all that their ardent author could have desired.

These acts of Seth, settled the suspicions of his captors into a certainty, and a closer surveillance was kept upon their refractory captive. No further opportunities were given him, and as he himself had expected this turn of matters, there was need for it upon his part. Although he had little reason to hope it, he did hope and believe that Haverland and Graham were upon the trail, and he felt that if the words intended for their eyes could only reach them, the fate of Ina and himself was determined.

The moon being at its full, and shining in unclouded splendor upon the forest, so lightened the way that the savages continued their flight—as it may now be well called—for an hour or two in the evening. They would have

61

probably gone farther, had it not been painfully evident that Ina was ready to give out. The old chief had given them imperative commands not to hasten her too much, and to rest when they saw she needed it. Accordingly, though they were brutal enough to insult her with menaces, they were of no avail, and, finally, they came to a reluctant halt for the night.

It will be necessary to understand the situation of these savages and their captives, in order to comprehend the events that followed.

A fire was started, and just within the circle of this, half-reclining upon the ground was Ina, with a heavy Indian shawl thrown around her. She had partaken of none of the food offered, and was already in a semi-conscious state. On either side of her was seated a vigilant savage, well armed and prepared for any emergency. Upon the opposite side was Seth, his feet firmly lashed together, while his hands were free. Two Indians were upon his right, and one upon his left. The remaining one took his station about a hundred yards on the back-trail.

Here, lying flat on his face, he silently waited for the approach of the enemy.

CHAPTER XIV.
IN THE ENEMY'S CAMP.
The savages, after starting the fire, allowed it to smolder and die out, for fear of guiding their enemies. Now this was the most fortunate thing that could have happened for their pursuers; for, in the first place, it burned long enough to give them a perfect knowledge of the position of Ina and Seth; and, when its light could no longer be of any assistance, but would materially injure their hopes, the Indians were kind enough to let it fade entirely out.

Before giving the signal, the hunter deemed it best to ascertain the whereabouts of the savage missing at the camp-fire. Leaving his rifle in the charge of Haverland, and cautioning them not to move, he crept stealthily forward. So silent and snake-like was his approach, that the savage lying directly in his path had not the slightest suspicion of his proximity. The first thing that attracted his attention was the thought that he heard a slight movement in front of him. Raising his head a few inches, he peered cautiously forward. Nothing meeting his keen vision he sunk back again.

The hunter and savage, both being on the ground, were in blank darkness, and although their forms, if standing on their feet, would have been plainly discernible, yet under the thick shadows of the undergrowth, they might have touched each other without knowing it. The hunter, however, as he lay, caught the outlines of the savage's head against the fading light of the fire behind him, as he raised it. This gave him a knowledge of his position and determined his own mode of action.

Without the least noise, he slid slowly forward until he was so close that he could actually hear the Indian's breath. Then he purposely made a slight movement. The Indian raised his head, and was gradually coming to his feet, when the hunter bounded like a dark ball forward, clutched him by the throat, and bearing him like a giant to the earth, drove his hunting knife again and again to the hilt in his heart. It was a fearful act, yet there was no hesitation upon the hunter's part. He felt that it must be done.

He loosened his grip upon his victim's throat, when there was not a spark of life left. Then casting his body to one side, he made his way back to his companions. Here, in a few words, he explained what had taken place. It was evident that the Indians were so cautious and alarmed, that the most consummate skill was required, to accomplish the work in hand.

Suddenly an ingenious plan occurred to Graham. It was to dress himself in the fallen Indian's dress, walk boldly into their camp, and be guided by circumstances. After a moment's consultation, it was acquiesced in by all. Haldidge made his way to where the savage lay, and hastily stripping him, returned with his garments. These Graham donned in a few moments, and was ready. It was agreed that he should walk leisurely among them, while Haverland and Haldidge would follow him, and remain nigh enough to be ready at a moment's warning. If discovered, he was to seize Ina and make off in the woods, while his two friends would rush forward, free Seth, and make an onslaught upon the others.

The fire was now so low, that Graham had little fear of exposing himself unless compelled to hold a conversation. The savages started as he came to view, but fortunately said nothing, as they supposed it to be their comrade. Graham walked leisurely to the almost dead fire, and seated himself by Seth. The savages continued placidly smoking their pipes.

"Ugh!" grunted Graham, peering into Seth's face. The latter started slightly, looked up, and understood all in a moment. Seth pointed to his feet; Graham nodded.

"Say, you, you was clever enough to tie up my feet, and, now just have the kindness to move 'em a little nearer the fire. Come, do, and I'll remember you in my will."

63

Graham mumbled something, and, stooping forward as he moved the feet slightly, dexterously cutting the thong at the same moment.

"Much obliged," said Seth; "that'll dew: needn't take no further trouble, you old painted heathen."

Graham felt that if he could now put Ina upon her guard, all would be necessary was—to act. But this was hardly possible. While ruminating upon the next step to be taken, an Indian addressed him in the Indian tongue. Here was a dilemma, and Graham was already meditating upon making the onslaught at once, when the ready wit of Seth came to his aid. Disguising most completely his voice, the eccentric fellow replied in the Indian tongue. This slight stratagem was executed so perfectly, that not a savage entertained the slightest suspicion that another than their dead comrade had spoken to them. Another question was put, but before Seth could reply, there came the startling cry of the whipporwil close at hand. All the savages sprang to their feet, and one held his tomahawk, ready to brain the captive Ina, in case they could not retain her. Another leaped toward Seth, but his surprise was great, when the man in turn sprang nimbly to his feet, and this surprise became unbounded, when, doubling himself like a ball, Seth struck him with tremendous force in the stomach, knocking him instantly senseless. Quick as thought, Graham felled the savage standing over Ina, and seizing her in his arms, plunged into the wood, setting up a loud shout at the same instant. The scene now became desperate. Haldidge and Haverland, fired almost to madness, rushed forward, and the former added his own yells to those of the savages. Ten minutes after, not an Indian was in sight. Finding it impossible to withstand this terrible onslaught, they fled precipitately, carrying with them several desperate wounds and feelings.

No lives were lost on either side, and not a wound worth mentioning was received by the assailants. The rout was complete.

But there was still danger, as the routed Indians would make all haste to the main body, and would in turn pursue the whites. This Haldidge remarked, as he struck into the forest, and called upon the others not to lose sight of him. There was danger of this, indeed.

"By gracious! yew, Haverland, things begin to look up," exclaimed Seth.

"Thank God!" responded the father, with a trembling voice.

Ina, for a few moments after her recapture, was so bewildered as not to comprehend the true state of affairs. Finally, she realized that she was in the arms of friends.

"Am I safe? Where is father?" she asked.

"Here, my dearest child," answered the parent, pressing her to his heart.

"Is mother and aunty safe?"

"Yes, all—all are safe, I trust now."

"And who are these, with you?"

"This is Haldidge, a dear friend of ours, to whom, under Heaven, your rescue is owing, and—"

"Just hold on, Alf, now, if you please; that's plenty," interrupted the hunter.

"Of course I did not mean to leave out Seth here, and—"

"No, by gracious, it wouldn't do, especially when you recollect how nice it was that me and Graham gave 'em the slip."

"You, and who?" eagerly asked Ina.

"Me and Mr. Graham—that fellow standing there—the one that has come out here to marry you. Haven't you heard of him?"

Ina stepped forward, and scrutinized the face before her.

"Don't you remember me?" asked Graham, pleasantly.

"Oh, is it you? I am so glad you are here," she repeated, placing both her hands in his, and looking up into his face.

"Now just see here," said Seth, stepping earnestly forward, "I 'bject to this. Cos why, you haven't the time to go into the sparking business, and if you do, why you'll be observed. I advise you to postpone it till you git home. What's the opinion of the audience?"

"Your suggestion is hardly necessary," laughed Graham. "The business you referred to, shall most certainly be deferred until a more convenient season."

65

"It gives me great pleasure," remarked Haverland, "to witness this reunion of friends, and I thank God that my dear child, so nearly lost forever, has been restored to me; but, there is another, whose heart is nearly broken, who should not be kept waiting, and there is a long distance between us and perfect safety, which should be shortened as rapidly and quickly as possible."

"That's the idea," added Haldidge, "it won't do to consider yourself safe till you are, and that isn't yet."

"Jest so, exactly, and consequently all fall into line of march."

Our friends now set out on a rapid walk homeward. As had been remarked, there was yet a long distance to be passed, and even now, while surrounded by darkness, it was reckless to halt or lag upon the way. Haldidge, as well as Seth, resolved that they should not pause until it was evident that Ina needed rest. Both well knew that the Mohawks would not yield up their captives, as long as there was a chance to regain them.

Seth's only fear now was that they would be pursued and overtaken by some of the savages. That this apprehension was well grounded, the events which we shall now record, will plainly show.

CHAPTER XV.
MANEUVERING AND SCHEMING.
Through the entire night, with now and then an occasional halt of a few minutes each, the fugitives—for they may now properly be termed such—continued their journey. When day broke, they halted in a small valley through which a small, sparkling stream made its way. On either side, it was surrounded by dark overhanging forest-trees and heavier undergrowth, through which none but the eagle eye of the hunter or savage, could discover their retreat.

Seth, when they first halted, made off in the woods, and in the course of a half-hour returned with a large fowl. The feathers were plucked from this, a fire kindled, and in a few moments it was cooked. It furnished all with a hearty, substantial and nourishing breakfast—what all needed. After this, a short consultation was held, when it was determined that they should halt for an hour or two. Several blankets were spread upon the green sward, as a bed for Ina, and in ten minutes she was sound asleep.

Our friends had decided upon making their homeward journey upon foot for several reasons, any of which was sufficient to influence them. In the first place, their course would be much shorter and more direct, and was really attended with less danger; and even if they desired to take to the river, there were no means at hand to do it.

"By gracious!" remarked Seth, after a few minute's deep thought, "I feel, boys, as though we're to run into a scrape before we get home. I tell yeou I do."

"And I do, too," added Haldidge. "I don't know why it is, and yet I believe there is reason for it. If there is any chance for them Mohawks to play the game of tit for tat, they'll do it; you can make up your mind to that."

"Do you think the chance is given them?" queried Haverland.

"I am afraid we can't help it, any way we choose to fix it."

"What do you mean? What do you refer to?"

"You see, them Ingins can't help knowing the way we'll have to take to reach home, and what is to hinder them from getting ahead of us and giving us a little trouble?"

"Nothing at all, that's the fact. Our utmost vigilance will be required at every step. Don't you think, Seth, that one of us should act in the capacity of scout?"

"I know it; not only one, but two. As soon as we start, I shall shoot ahead and pilot you along, while one of you must flourish in the rear to announce any new visitors. This is the only way we can ever expect to move along with dignity."

"What course do you suppose the savages will take?" asked Graham.

"I guess they ain't in the neighborhood, though it's darned hard to tell where they are. You can make up your mind that they'll show themselves before we get any great distance ahead. They'll be dodging round in the woods till they find out where we are, and then they'll use their wits to draw us into ambush, and I can tell yeou, too, that cuter ones than we have walked right into the infarnal things."

An hour later, when preparations were making for resuming their journey, Ina awoke. She was greatly refreshed by the sleep thus obtained, and the others felt cheered and hopeful at the prospect of a rapid march for the day.

67

The burden and responsibility of this small band of adventurers naturally devolved upon Haldidge and Seth. Haverland, although a thorough hunter and woodsman, had had little or no experience in Indian warfare, and accordingly showed himself to be devoid of that suspicious watchfulness which makes up the success of the frontier ranger. As for Graham, he was suspicious enough, but he lacked also the great teacher—experience. Seth and Haldidge thus thrown together, rapidly consulted and determined in all cases the precautionary measures to be adopted. In the present instance, it was decided that Haldidge should linger some hundred yards in the rear, and use all the opportunities thus afforded of watching the actions or approach of their enemies. The same duty was imposed upon Seth, with the additional certainty upon his part, that the entire safety of the company rested with him.

Haverland and Graham generally walked side by side, with Ina between them, and as watchful as though they had none but themselves to depend upon. They seldom indulged in conversation, except now and then to exchange a few words or inquiries.

As Seth Jones was well satisfied in his own mind, that the part of danger was held by him, we will follow his adventures. After emerging from the valley, in which the whites had encamped, their way for a considerable distance led through the unbroken forest, without hill or vale, and pretty thickly crowded with bushy, yielding undergrowth. Had a person chanced to cross the path of Seth, the only evidence he would have had of the presence of a human being, would have been the snapping of a twig now and then, or the flitting of his form like a shadow from tree to tree, and perhaps the shrill, bird-like whistle as he signaled to those in the rear.

Through the forenoon, nothing occurred to excite suspicion upon his part, but at the period mentioned, he arrived at a point where his alarm was excited at once. The place offered such advantages for an Indian ambush, that he gave the signal for those behind to halt, and determined to make a thorough reconnoissance of the whole locality before passing through it. The spot referred to, had the appearance of having formerly been the bed of some large-sized lake, the water of which having dried up years before, left a rich, productive soil which was now covered over with the rankest undergrowth and vegetation. Not a tree of any size appeared. The hollow, or valley, was so much depressed that from the stand-point of Seth, he obtained a perfect view of the whole portion. It was of about a third of a mile in breadth, and perhaps a couple of miles in length.

Seth stood a long time, running his eye over it, scanning every spot where it seemed likely an enemy might lurk. Hardly a point escaped his keen vision.

68

It was while he stood thus, eagerly scanning the valley, that his looks were suddenly attracted toward a point near the center of the valley, from which a faint, bluish wreath of smoke was curling upward. This puzzled our friend greatly. He possessed the curious, investigating habits so generally ascribed to his race, and his curiosity was wonderfully excited by this occurrence. That there was some design in it, not understood yet, he was well satisfied, and he determined that, before allowing those behind him to venture into the valley, he would gain all knowledge possible of it. His first step was to take his own trail backward until he reached Haverland and Graham, to whom he imparted his intention. This done, he set forward again.

Having arrived at the point where he had first discovered this suspicious appearance, he paused again for further consideration. The smoke was still visible, rising very slowly in the clear air, and making so slight an appearance that even his experienced eye searched a long time for it. Seth watched for a while, until he felt that he could not understand the meaning of it without venturing into the valley. This conclusion arrived at, he hesitated no longer, but descended and entered at once the luxuriant growth.

When fairly within it, he made a detour to the right, so as to pass around the fire, and to avoid the path that one unsuspicious of danger would be apt to follow. As he made his way slowly and cautiously forward, he paused at intervals and listened intently. Sometimes he bent his ear to the ground and lay for minutes at a time. But as yet, not the slightest sound had been heard. Finally he judged that he must be near the fire that had excited his apprehensions. The snapping of a burning ember guided him, and a few minutes later he stood within sight of it.

Here he met a sight that chilled him with horror!

Some wretched human being was bound to a tree and had been burned to death. He was painted black as death, his scalped head drooped forward, so that, from where Seth stood, it was impossible to distinguish his features; but he saw enough to make him shudder at the awful fate he had so narrowly escaped. Every vestige of flesh was burnt off to the knees, and the bones, white and glistening, dangled to the crisp and blackened members above! The hands, tied behind, had passed through the fire unscathed, but every other part of the body was literally roasted! The smoke in reality was the smoke from this human body, and the stench which was now horrible, had been noticed by Seth long before he suspected the cause.

69

"Heavens and earth!" he muttered to himself, "this is the first time I ever saw a person burnt at the stake, and I hope to God it will be the last time. Can he be a white man?"

After some cautious maneuvering, he gained a point from which he could obtain a view of the face, and he experienced considerable relief when he discovered that it was not a white man. He was probably some unfortunate Indian, belonging to a hostile tribe, who had been captured by his enemies, and upon whom they had thus wreaked their vengeance. Whether he was a Mohawk or the member of another tribe, it was impossible for Seth, under the circumstances, to tell. But what was singular and unaccountable to Seth, was, that there appeared to be no other savages in the vicinity. He knew it was not their custom to leave a prisoner thus, and the very fact of their being absent upon the present occasion, made him doubly cautious and suspicious.

It was while he stood meditating upon the terrible scene before him, that he was startled by the report of Haldidge's rifle. He was satisfied that it was his as it was from that direction, and he could not be mistaken in the report. He had noticed it during the conflict the night before, as having a peculiar sound entirely different from either his own or the savages'. This was a new source of wonder and perplexity. He was completely puzzled by the extraordinary turn affairs were taking. Some unusual cause must have discharged Haldidge's rifle. What it was he could only conjecture.

Still doubtful and cautious, he determined to reconnoiter his own position before returning. Stooping almost to the earth, he made his way stealthily around to the opposite side of the fire. Here he stretched out flat upon the earth and bent his ear to the ground. A faint tremor was heard. He raised his head and heard the brushing of some body through the wood. The next moment, five Mohawk warriors, in all the horrid panoply of war paint, stepped into the open space in front of the Indian who had been burnt at the stake.

The report of the rifle appeared to be the cause of the apprehension among them. They conversed earnestly in a low tone at first, gesticulating violently, without noticing in the least the heart-sickening spectacle before them. Seth was satisfied that they had no suspicions of his own proximity, for they gradually spoke louder until he managed to overhear the most of what they said. As he expected, it was the rifle report. They seemed to understand that it had not been discharged by one of their own number, and were afraid that their presence had been discovered. Seth learned further that there were at least a dozen Indians in the neighborhood, every one of whom were led thither by the one object.

Consequently he must have missed the others entirely in his movements, or else they were in the rear and had been discovered by Haldidge. That the latter was the case, seemed more than probable. A collision in all probability had occurred between them and the hunter, and Seth felt that his presence was needed. Accordingly he turned to retrace his steps.

His presence was indeed required, for danger, dark and threatening, surrounded the little band of whites.

CHAPTER XVI.
IN WHICH A HUNTER'S NERVES ARE TESTED.

In the morning when our friends started upon their day's march, Haldidge, as said, fell behind in order to guard against surprise from this direction. Although expecting as little as did Seth any demonstration from this quarter, still he was too much of a backwoodsman to allow himself to lose any of his usual suspicion and watchfulness. Sometimes he would take his back trail for a long distance, and then wander off to the right or left of it for perhaps a mile or more. By this means, he kept a continual watch not only upon the trail itself but upon the neighborhood for a long distance around it, and, in case of pursuit, made so many and conflicting tracks, that it could not but puzzle and delay their enemies.

Near noon, and at the very moment that Seth paused to take a survey of the suspicious valley-like depression, and when not more than a furlong in the rear, Haldidge caught sight of three Indians just ahead of him. They were sitting upon the ground, in perfect silence, and seemingly waiting for the approach of some one. The hunter found himself as much perplexed, as was Seth to account for what he saw. Whether it was some stratagem to entrap himself or not he could not tell, but before venturing farther, he made up his mind to gain a further knowledge of their intentions.

Haldidge had one formidable difficulty to contend with: the wood at this particular spot was open, and almost devoid of the protecting undergrowth, so that it was about impossible to approach them closer without discovering himself to them. He noticed lying a short distance behind them a large, heavy log, apparently much decayed. In fact this was so near them, that could he gain it, he could overhear every thing said. He had a slight knowledge of the Mohawk tongue—not enough to converse in it—but still enough to understand the drift of a conversation. Accordingly he determined to reach the spot at all hazards.

Haldidge desired, if possible, to communicate with Haverland and warn him of the proximity of danger. To do this, it was necessary to make a long detour, and upon further consideration he decided not to attempt it. Lying flat upon his face, he worked himself toward the log mentioned, keeping it between himself and the Indians, and approaching as silently and steadily as a snake. So cautiously and carefully was it done, that it required at least twenty minutes to reach it, and all this time, the Indians maintained the same unbroken silence. At length, the concealment was reached, and the hunter noticed with pleasure that it was hollow. He lost no time in entering it, where, coiling himself up in as small a space as possible, he took himself to listening. As if to completely favor him, there was a small rent in the log, through which even the whisper of the savages could be heard, and which also admitted a thin ray of light.

Here Haldidge cramped himself up and listened intently. But not a word was exchanged between the Indians, who remained as motionless as statues. In the course of a few minutes he heard a footfall upon the leaves, and a second after several savages seated themselves upon the very log in which he had concealed himself! He judged that there were at least a half dozen. Those whom he had first seen appeared to have risen, and, meeting the others, they had all seated themselves upon the log together.

They immediately commenced conversing in so low and guttural tones, that their deep base voices communicated their tremor to the log. Haldidge started as he soon learned that they were conversing about himself and the three fugitives. Of Seth they seemed to have no knowledge. He discovered that they had lain in ambush a short distance ahead to entrap Haverland, Graham, and Ina, and they were debating how he should be disposed of. They knew that he was acting in the capacity of scout and sentinel, and were fearful that he might detect the ambush, or at least escape it himself.

At this point, one of the Indians, probably impelled by some whim, stooped and looked into the log. Haldidge knew from the darkness thus occasioned, that one of them was peering in it, and he scarcely breathed for a few seconds. But the face was removed, and the hollow being dark within—the small rent being upon the opposite side of the hunter—the savage felt reassured and resumed the conversation.

But Haldidge was doomed to have a trial of his nerves, of which he little dreamed. When he entered the log, it was head foremost, so that his feet were toward the opening, and his face was in the dim light beyond. He judged the rotten cavity extended several feet further back; but, as there was no necessity for entering farther, he did not attempt to explore it. It was while he lay thus, his whole soul bent to the one act of listening, that he was startled by the deadly warning of a rattlesnake! He comprehended the truth in an instant. There was one of these reptiles in the log beyond him!

It is difficult to imagine a more fearful situation than the hunter's at this moment. He was literally environed by death; for it was at his head, his feet, and above him, and there was no escape below. He had just learned that his death was one of the objects of the Indians, so that to back out into their clutches

72

would be nothing less than committing suicide. To remain where he was, would be to disregard the second and last warning of the coiled rattlesnake. What was to be done? Manifestly nothing but to die like a man. Haldidge decided to risk the bite of the rattlesnake!

Despite himself, the hunter felt that the reptile was exerting its horrible fascination over him. Its small eyes, gleaming like tiny, yet fiery stars, seemed to emit a magnetic ray—thin, pointed and palpable, that pierced right into his brain. There was a malignant subtlety—an irresistible magnetism. Now the small, glittering point of light seemed to recede, then to approach and expand, and then to wave and undulate all around him. Sometimes that bright, lightning-like ray would shiver and tremble, and then straighten out with metal-like rigidity, and insinuate itself into his very being like the invisible point of a spear.

There was a desire on the part of Haldidge to shake off this influence, which wrapped him like a mantle. There was the desire, we say, and yet there was a languid listlessness—a repugnance to making the effort. The feeling was something similar to that produced by a powerful opiate, when we are first recovering from it. There was that dim consciousness—that indistinct knowledge of the outer world—that certainty, that we can break the bond that holds us, by one vigorous effort, and yet the same sluggish indifference that prevents the attempt.

Haldidge drew his breath faintly and slowly, yielding more and more to that fatal subtle influence. He knew he was charmed, and yet he couldn't help it. It was now impossible to shake off that weight which pressed him down like an incubus. That outer world—so to speak—had now receded, and he was in another, from which he could not return without help beside his own. He seemed to be moving, flitting, sinking, and rising, through the thin air, borne upward and downward, hither and thither, on a wing of fire. The spell was complete. That extraordinary power which instinct holds over reason—that wonderful superiority which a reptile sometimes shows he can exert over man, the snake now held over the hunter.

At this point, from some cause or other, one of the savages struck the log a violent blow with his hatchet. Haldidge heard it. He drew a long breath, closed his eyes, and when he reopened them, looked down at his hands upon which his chin had been resting.

The charm was broken! the hunter had shaken off the fatal spell!

Like the knocking at the gate in Macbeth, which dispels the dark, awful world of gloom in which the murderers have been moving and living, and ushers in our own world, with all its hurrying tide of human life and passions; so this blow of the Indian's tomahawk broke the subtle, magnetic spell of the

73

serpent, and lifted the heavy mantle-like influence which wrapped Haldidge in its folds.

He looked downward, and determined not to raise his eyes again, for he knew the same power would again rise above him. The serpent, seemingly conscious of its loss of influence, rattled once more, and prepared to strike. Haldidge stirred not a muscle; in fact, he had scarcely moved since entering the log. But the snake did not strike. The continued, death-like stillness of the hunter, evidently seemed to the reptile to be death itself. He coiled and uncoiled himself several times, and then lifting his head, crawled directly over his neck and body, and passed out of the log! Here he was killed by the Indians.

Now that the hunter was himself again, he prepared for further action. The Indians had arisen from the log and were at some distance. He could hear the mumbling of their voices, but could not distinguish their words. After awhile these ceased, and he heard no more.

Haldidge was now filled with apprehension for the others. He had enough faith in the power and cunning of Seth to feel pretty confident that he would neither lead any one into ambush or fall into one himself, let it be prepared as skillfully as it might be; but then he could know nothing of the Indians in the rear, who might surprise Haverland and Graham at any moment.

The hunter at length grew so restless and uneasy that he emerged from his hiding-place as rapidly and silently as possible. He looked cautiously around, but no savage was in sight. Filled with the most painful apprehensions, he hastened through the wood, avoiding the trail of his friends, however, and finally came in sight of them. Before making himself known he concluded to reconnoiter the place. While doing so, he saw the head of an Indian rise slowly above a bush, and peer over at the unconscious whites. Without losing a moment, he raised his rifle, took a quick but sure aim, and fired. Then calling out to Haverland and Graham, he sprang for an instant into view.

"Make for cover!" he shouted; "the Indians are upon us!"

In an instant, every one of the whites was invisible.

CHAPTER XVII.
ENCOMPASSED BY DANGER.

At the first warning of Haldidge, Haverland comprehended the threatened danger in an instant. Catching Ina in his arms, he sprang into the wood, sheltering himself behind a tree so quickly that Ina, till that moment, did not comprehend the meaning of the startling movements around her.

"What is it, father?" she whispered.

"Keep quiet, daughter, and don't move."

She said no more but shrank beneath his sheltering form, believing that his strong arm was capable of protecting her against any foe, however formidable.

Graham, at the alarm, had leaped toward Haldidge, and the two sheltered themselves within a few feet of each other. The shot of the hunter had been fatal, for that yell, which the North American Indian, like the animal, gives when he receives his death-wound, was heard, and the fall had also reached his ears.

Minute after minute passed away and nothing further was heard of the savages. This silence was as full of meaning, and as dangerous as any open demonstration upon the part of the Indian. What new plan they might be concocting was a mystery to all but themselves. At length Graham ventured to speak:

"What do you suppose they're up to, Haldidge?"

"Hatching some devilish plot, I expect."

"It seems it requires a good while to do it."

"Don't get impatient; they'll show themselves in time."

"Have you any idea of their number?"

"There were something like a half-dozen prowling around."

"There is one less now at any rate."

"I suppose so; but there's enough left to occasion a little trouble at least. Where did Alf go with the gal?"

"Off yonder, a short distance. Hadn't we better get closer together?"

"No; I don't know as there is any necessity for it. We're as safe, drawn up in this style, as in any other I can imagine."

"I am afraid, Haldidge, they will make an attempt to surround us. In such a case, wouldn't Haverland be in great peril?"

"They can't get around him without running their heads in range with our rifles, and Alf is a man who'll be pretty sure to discover such a trick without any help."

"Where can Seth be?"

"Not very far off; that shot of mine will be pretty sure to bring him."

"Haldidge, how was it that you discovered these Mohawks? Did you know of their presence before you fired?"

"Yes, long before. I've an idea they've been tracking you for an hour or two."

"Why, then, was their attack deferred?"

"They have made no attack, remember. I don't believe they had any such intention. There is an ambush somewhere ahead that they have laid, and it was their idea to walk you into that."

"What was their notion in watching us so closely."

"They were hunting for me, for I heard them say as much, and, I suppose, in case you didn't walk into their trap, why they were going to make the attack."

"Can it be that Seth has fallen into the snare?" asked Graham in anxious tones.

"No, sir; such a thing can't be. He isn't such a fool as that amounts to. He is making himself generally useful; you can make your mind to that. He is a smart chap, for all he is the most awkward, long-legged, gawky person I ever came across."

"I am puzzled to know who he is. It seems to me that he is only playing a part. Several times in conversing with him, he has used language such as none but a scholar and polished gentleman would use. At others and most of the time, he uses that ungainly mode of expression, which in itself, is laughable. At any rate, whoever he may be, he is a friend, and the interest which he takes in the safety of Haverland and his family is as efficient as it is singular."

"Maybe the interest is in Ina," said Haldidge with a sly look.

"I understand you, but you are mistaken. He has assured me as much. No; there seems nothing of that feeling at all in him. He loves her as he would a child, but no more."

"How was it that he made that awkward tumble into the Indians hands, when they gave you such a hard run for it?"

"That was all through my own blundering. He was cautious enough, but I became so impatient and careless that I precipitated him into the danger which would have been fatal to any one else. It was no fault of his."

"I am glad to hear it, for it seemed odd to me."

This conversation which we have recorded, it must not be supposed, was not carried on in an ordinary tone, and with that earnestness which would have lessened their habitual caution. It was in whispers, and hardly once during its progress did the two look at each other. Sometimes they would not speak for several minutes, and then exchange but a single question and answer.

It was now toward the middle of the afternoon, and it became pretty evident that the night would have to be spent in this neighborhood.

"I do hope that Seth will make his appearance before dark," remarked Graham.

"Yes; I hope he will, for it will be dangerous when we can't see him."

"He must be aware of the threatened danger."

"Yes; I am pretty confident that he is not very distant."

"Hallo! what's that?" whispered Graham.

"Ah! keep quiet; there's something going on there."

A death-like silence reigned for a few minutes; then, a slight rustling was heard close by Haldidge, and as he turned his alarmed gaze toward it, the form of Seth Jones rose to his feet beside him.

"Where did you come from?" asked Graham in astonishment.

"I have been watching you. In a little trouble, eh?"

"We've found out we've got neighbors."

"They're not very nigh neighbors leastways."

"What do you mean?"

"There isn't one in a quarter of a mile."

Haldidge and Graham looked at the speaker in astonishment.

"I tell you, it's so. Hallo, Haverland!" he called, stepping out from his concealment. "Come out here; there is nothing to be afraid of."

The manner of the speaker was singular, but the others well knew that he was not one to expose either himself or others to danger, and accordingly all gathered around him.

"Are you not running great risk?" asked Haverland, still experiencing some slight misgivings at stepping upon a spot which he well knew was so dangerous a short time before.

"No, sir; I reckon you needn't be at all skeerish, for if there was any danger of them Mohawks, I wouldn't be standing here."

"It's getting toward night, Seth, and we should make up our minds at once as to what we are going to do or how we are going to spend it."

"Can you shoot a gun?" asked Seth suddenly, of Ina.

"I don't believe you can beat me," she answered lightly.

"That is good."

So saying, he stepped into the bushes, where the dead body of the Indian was lying. Stooping over him, he removed the rifle from his rigid grasp, took his bullet-pouch and powder, and handed them to Ina.

"Now, there are five of us, all well armed," said he, "and if any of them infarnal Mohawks gets ahead of us, we all desarve red night-caps for it."

"How are we to prevent it, when there seems to be ten times our number following us?" asked Haverland.

"The way on it is this ere: there is about a dozen trying to sarcumvent us. They're now ahead of us, and have laid an ambush for us. If we can pass that

78

ambush we're safe as if we was home fair and sure. And there must be no if about it, for that ambush must be passed to-night."

CHAPTER XVIII.
GETTING OUT OF THE WILDERNESS.

Night, dark and gloomy, slowly settled over the forest. Nothing was heard save the dull soughing of the wind through the tree-tops, or the occasional howl of the wolf in the distance, or perhaps the near scream of the panther. Heavy, tumultuous clouds were wheeling through the sky, rendering the inky darkness doubly intense, and shrouding even the clearings in impenetrable gloom.

By and by, the distant rumble of thunder came faintly through the air, and then a quivering fork of fire, like a stream of blood, trembled upon the edge of the dark storm-cloud for an instant. The heavy clouds, growing darker and more awful, poured forward until they seemed to concentrate in the western sky, where they towered aloft like some old embattled castle. The thunder grew heavier, until it sounded like the rolling of chariot wheels over the courts of heaven, and the red streams of liquid fire streamed down the dark walls of the Storm Castle. Now and then the subtle element flamed out into a dazzling, instantaneous flash, and the bolt burst overhead.

"Keep close to me and step light, for I tell you there's enough lightning."

Seth had thoroughly reconnoitered the valley to which we have referred, and had found, as he expected, that there was an ambush laid for them. There was a sort of foot-path, apparently worn by the passing of wild animals, which nearly crossed the valley. It was here that the Indians supposed the fugitives would be entrapped, until the death of a too daring member of their party led them to suspect that their intentions were discovered.

The little band was hours in crossing this valley. Seth, with an almost inaudible "sh!" would often pause, and they would stand for many anxious minutes listening intently for the dreaded danger. Then they would resume their march, stepping with painful slowness.

It was at least three hours after the fugitives commenced this journey, and when Seth judged that he must be nearly through it, that he suddenly discovered he was walking in the very path he had striven so carefully to avoid. He was considerably startled at this, and left at once.

"Sh! down!" he whispered, turning his face behind him.

They were not ten feet from the path, when they all sank quietly to the earth. Footsteps were now audible to all. The darkness was too profound to discern any thing, but all heard their enemies almost near enough to touch them with the outstretched hand.

The situation of our friends was imminently perilous. The Mohawks were not passing along the path, as at first supposed, but evidently searching it! Haldidge and Seth felt that they could not be aware of their proximity, and yet they knew a discovery was unavoidable.

Seth Jones rose to his feet so silently, that even Haldidge, who was within a foot of him, did not hear a rustle. He then touched Haverland's ear with his mouth, and whispered:

"Scatter with the gal as quick as lightning, for they must find us out in a minute."

Haverland lifted Ina in his strong arm—she needed no caution, and stepped forward. It was impossible not to make some noise, when the wet bushes brushed against them. The savages heard it and started cautiously forward. They evidently suspected it was the fugitives, and had no suspicion that any one was lingering in the rear. The first warning Seth had, was of a savage running plump against him.

"Beg your pardon, I didn't see you," exclaimed Seth, as each bounded backward. "Curse you," he muttered, "I only wish I could sight you for a minute."

Seth, Haldidge and Graham were now maneuvering against some five or six Indians. Had a bright flash of lightning illuminated the scene, just at this time, it is probable that all would have laughed outright, at the attitude and movements of themselves. The Indians, upon finding how near they were to their deadliest enemies, immediately bounded backward several yards, in order to avoid a too sudden collision with them. The three whites did precisely the same thing—each in his own characteristic way. Seth leaped to one side, crouched down in his usual panther-like manner, and with his rifle in his left, and his knife in his right hand, waited until he could settle in his mind the precise spot upon which one of the savages was standing, before making a lunge at him.

It would be tedious to narrate the artifices and stratagem resorted to by these two opposing forces. Simon Kenton and Daniel Boone, once reached the opposite aides of the Ohio river at the same moment, and at the same time, each became aware of the presence of another person upon the other side. These two old hunters and acquaintances reconnoitered for over twenty-four hours, before they discovered that they were friends. For nearly two hours, the Mohawks and the whites maneuvered with the most consummate skill against each other. Now retreating and leading, dodging and eluding, each striving to lead the other into some trap that was as skillfully avoided, until, judging that Haverland was safe, Seth concluded to retreat himself accordingly, he cautiously withdrew, and ten minutes later, found himself upon the outermost edge of the valley.

Ten minutes after Seth departed, Haldidge moved off, of course unknown to himself, in precisely the same direction. Graham soon adopted the same course. They all came out of the dangerous valley within twenty feet of each other. It took them some time before they came together; but, as each suspected the identity of the other, this did not require as long as it otherwise would.

"Now, boys," whispered Seth, "I cac'late we're out of the Valley of Death. Best give it a wide berth, is the private opinion of Seth Jones."

"But how about Haverland?" asked Graham.

"I think they must have come out near that point," replied the other.

"Let us move round then, and we've got to be spry, for daylight can't be far off, and I'm thinking as how them Ingins will find out that we've absconded; and my gracious! won't they feel cheap?"

Just as the light of morning appeared in the east, they came upon Haverland, and resumed their journey. No halt was made for breakfast, for they were all too anxious to get forward upon their way. In the course of an hour or so, they struck a sort of path, made by the passage of wild animals, which, besides being so hardened as to conceal their trail, was easily traveled.

Seth and Haldidge were too experienced woodsmen to relax their vigilance. They maintained the same duties as before, the former taking it upon himself to lead the way through the wilderness, and the latter to guard against danger from behind. The settlement toward which they were so anxiously hastening, was still several days distant, and to reach it, it was necessary to cross a river of considerable breadth. This river was reached by Seth at noon.

"By gracious! I forgot about this!" he exclaimed to himself. "Wonder if the gal can swim? If she can't, how are we going to get her over? Put her on a chip, I s'pose, and let the breeze blow her across: the rest of us can swim, in course."

A few minutes later, our friends stood consulting upon the bank of the stream.

This consultation ended in active preparations for crossing on a raft. Hunting up material for constructing a raft now was the order of the hour. This was work of extreme difficulty. They had no instruments except their hunting-knives, and these were little better than nothing. Large, rotten limbs were broken from the trees, and placed together by Haverland, who took upon himself the task of lashing them with withes, while the others collected wood.

Haldidge went up the river, and Seth and Graham went down. Graham soon noticed a large, half-decayed log, lying partly in the water. "Just the thing, exactly! Why it's a raft itself. This will save further trouble. Let us launch it at once, and float it up to the spot," he said, delightedly.

The two approached it, stooped, and were in the very act of lifting it into the water, when Seth suddenly removed his shoulder, and arose to the upright position.

"Come, give a lift," said Graham.

"Graham, I guess I wouldn't take the log, I don't think it will answer."

"Won't answer? Why not? In the name of common sense, give some reason."

"Let that log alone! Do you understand?"

Graham looked up, and started at the appearance of Seth. His eyes fairly scintillated and he seemed ready to spring upon him, for daring to utter a word of dispute.

"Come along with me!" commanded Seth, in a voice hoarse with passion.

It wouldn't do to disregard that command; and, taking up his rifle, Graham lost no time in obeying it. But he wondered greatly whether Seth was suddenly become crazy or foolish. He followed him a short distance, and then hastened up beside him. Seeing that his face had recovered its usual expression, he gained courage and asked what he meant by such commands?

"Didn't you take notice that that log was holler?"

"I believe it was, although I did not examine it closely."

"Wal, if you had examined it closely or even loosely, so that you took a peep into the log, you'd have seen a big Mohawk curled up there snug and nice!"

"Is it possible! How came you to see him?"

"The minute I seed the log was holler, I had my s'picions that there might be something or other in it, and I made up my mind that we shouldn't undertake to lift it till I knowd how it was. When I come to look closer, I knowed thar was something sure enough, for the way the bark was scratched at the mouth showed that plain enough. It wouldn't do, you see, to stoop down and peep in, for like as not the redskin would blaze away smack into my face. So I jest dropped my cap, and, as I stooped down to pick it up, I kind of slewed one eye 'round over my shoulder, and, as sure as blazes, I seen a big moccasin! I did, by gracious! I then proceeded to argufy the question; and, after considerable discussion, both in the affirmative and negative, I came unanimously to the conclusion that as I'd seen an Injin's foot, if I'd foller it up, I'd be pretty sure to find the Injin himself; and, moreover, also, if there was one Injin about, you could make up your mind that there are plenty more not far off. By gracious! If I hadn't looked a little ramparageous, you wouldn't have let go that log so very quick, eh?"

"No; you alarmed me considerably. But what is to be done?"

"The cowards are poking around the woods, fixing out some plan to ambush us again. They've no idea we've smelt the rat that's brewing in the bud, and they're too cowardly to show their faces until they find they've got to, or let us slip."

"Shall we tell Haverland?"

"No; I will let Haldidge know it, if he hasn't found it out already. The raft has got to be made, and we must keep on at it till it's finished, as though we knowed every thing was right. Keep still now, or Alf will notice our talking."

They were so close to the woodman that they changed their conversation.

"No material?" asked Haverland, looking up.

"It's rather scarce down where we've been," replied Graham.

"Shan't I help you?" asked Ina, looking up archly.

83

"I guess we won't need your help as Haldidge seems to have enough already."

The hunter at this moment approached, bending under the weight of two heavy limbs. These were instantly lashed together, but it was found that the raft was much too weak and light, and more stuff was necessary before it would even float Ina. Accordingly, Haldidge plunged into the wood again. Seth walked beside him until they were a few yards away, when he asked:

"Do you understand?"

"What?" asked the hunter in astonishment.

"Over there," answered Seth, jerking his thumb over his shoulder toward the log mentioned.

"Redskins?"

"I rather guess so."

"I smelt them, awhile ago. You'd better go back and watch Alf. I'll get enough wood. Danger!"

"No; they'll try some game; look out for yourself."

With this, Seth turned on his heel and rejoined Haverland. Graham was a short distance away cutting withes, which the woodman was as busily using. As Seth came up he noticed Ina. She was sitting upon the ground a few feet from her father, and her attention seemed wholly absorbed with some thing down the stream. Seth watched her closely.

"Isn't that a log yonder?" she asked.

Seth looked in the direction indicated. With no small degree of astonishment, he saw the identical tree which he and Graham disputed over, afloat in the river. This awoke his apprehensions and he signaled at once for Haldidge.

"What's the row?" asked the hunter as he came up.

Seth gave his head a toss down stream, by way of reply, and added, "Don't let 'em see you're watching it, for it might scare 'em."

Nevertheless Haldidge turned square around and took a long, searching look at the suspicious object.

"What do you make of it?"

"Them Mohawks are the biggest fools I ever heard of, to think that such an old trick as that can amount to any thing."

"What trick do you mean?" asked Haverland.

"Why, you see that log yonder, half sunk in the water, that we are all looking at? Well, there are four or five Mohawks behind that, waiting for us to launch our raft."

"Maybe it's nothing more than a floating tree or log," said the woodman.

"Y-e-s," drawled the hunter sarcastically, "maybe so; I s'pose a log would be very apt to float up stream, wouldn't it?"

"Why, is it approaching?" asked Graham.

"Not very fast," answered Seth, "for I guess it's hard work for them fellers to swim up stream. Ah! by gracious! I understand the game. Look; don't you see it's farther out than it was? They're going to get as near the middle as they can, and so close to us that when we undertake to cross, the current will carry us right down plump against 'em, when they'll rise up in their wrath and devour us. Fact, as sure as you live."

"We might as well understand matters at once," added Haldidge. "The plan of the Indians is undoubtedly the same as Seth suggests. In crossing, we cannot help drifting downward, and they are trying to locate themselves so as to make a collision between us. But they will make no attack until we are in the water. So you may keep at work upon the raft, Alf, without any fear, while Seth and I reconnoiter. Come, Graham, you may as well go along with us. Let us enter the wood separately at first, and we'll come together as soon as we can get out of sight. Act as though we didn't suspicion any thing, and I'll wager my rifle here against your hat that we'll outwit the cowards after all."

The three entered the wood as proposed. After going a few yards they came together again.

"Now," whispered Seth, "by gracious! you will see fun. Follow close, boys, and keep shady."

Being now fairly within the wood, they proceeded in a direction parallel with the course of the river, using extreme caution, for it was more than probable some of the Indian scouts were secreted in the wood. Keeping entirely

85

away from the river until Seth judged they were below the suspicious log, they approached it. A reckless move, at this point, would have been fatal. Fortunately, there was a species of grass growing from the wood out to a considerable distance in the water. Through this, they made their way much after the fashion of snakes. Seth, as usual, was in front, and it struck Graham that he absolutely slid over the ground without any exertion on his part.

In a moment, they were down to the river's brink. They now slowly raised their heads and peered over and through the grass out into the river. The log was a short distance above, and they had a perfect view of the side which was opposite to Haverland. Not a sign of an Indian was visible. The tree seemed as if anchored in the middle of the stream.

"There is something there!" whispered Graham.

"—sh! keep quiet and watch and you'll see!" admonished Seth.

A moment more, and the log apparently, without any human agency, slightly changed its position. As it did so, Graham saw something glisten on the top of it. He was at a loss to understand what it meant, and turned inquiringly toward Haldidge. The latter had his keen eye fixed upon it, and there was a grim, exulting smile upon his face. He motioned for Graham to preserve silence.

As our hero turned his gaze once more toward the river, he saw that the log was still further into the stream. Something like polished metal was seen glistening even brighter than before. He looked carefully, and in a moment saw that there were several rifles resting upon the surface of it.

While gazing and wondering where the owners of these weapons could conceal themselves, the water suddenly seemed to part on the side of the log toward them, and the bronzed face of an Indian rose to view. Up, up, it went, until the shoulders were out of the water, when he remained stationary a moment, and peered over the log at Haverland. Seemingly satisfied, he quietly sank down into the water again; but Graham noticed that he did not disappear beneath the surface, where it appeared he had hitherto kept himself, nestled in so close to the log that almost any one would have supposed he was a part of it. His head resembled exactly a large black knot in the wood. Graham now noticed also that there were two other protuberances, precisely similar to the first. The conclusion was certain. There were three fully armed Mohawks concealed behind the log, who were doing their utmost to steal unawares upon the fugitives.

"Just exactly one apiece, as sure as you live," exclaimed Seth exultingly. "Get ready each of you for your man. Graham, take the one nearest this way;

you the next one, Haldidge, and I'll pick off the last one in the genuine style. Get ready quick, for I've got to hurrah over the way things is coming round."

The three pointed their deathly instruments toward the unsuspicious savages. Each took a long, deliberate, and certain aim.

"Now, then, together—fire!"

Simultaneously the three rifles flashed, but that of Seth missed fire. The others sped true to their aim. Two yells of deathly agony broke upon the air, and one of the savages sprang half his entire length out of the water, and then sank like lead to the bottom. The other clung quivering to the log for a moment, and then loosening his hold, disappeared beneath the water.

"Thunder and blazes!" exclaimed Seth, springing to his feet, "hand me your rifle, Graham. Something is the matter with mine, and that other imp will get away. Quick! hand it here!"

He took the rifle and commenced loading it as rapidly as possible, keeping his eye upon the Indian who now was swimming desperately for the other bank.

"Is yer iron loaded, Haldidge?" he asked.

"No; I've been watching you and that chap's doubling, to see who'll get the best, so long, that I didn't think of it."

"Load again, for s'posen this gun should miss fire too, he'd get off then sure. Wal, my stars! if he isn't coming out now."

The Indian, as if scorning the danger, rose slowly from the water, and walked leisurely toward the shelter of the wood.

"Now, my fine feller, see if you can dodge this."

Seth once more aimed at the retreating Indian, and this time pulled the trigger; but to his unutterable chagrin, the rifle flashed in the pan! Before Haldidge could finish loading his gun, and before Seth could even reprime his, the Indian had disappeared in the wood.

"By the hokey-pokey! what's got into the guns?" exclaimed Seth in a perfect fury. "That's twice I've been fooled! Worse'n two slaps in the face by a purty woman, I'll swow. Hallo! what's that?"

The discharge of a rifle across the river had sent the bullet so close to him as to whisk off a tuft of his long sandy hair!

"By gracious! that was pretty well done," he exclaimed, scratching his head as though he was slightly wounded.

"Look out, for heaven's sake! Get down!" called Graham, seizing him by the skirt of his hunting dress, and jerking him downward.

"Don't know but what it is the best plan," replied the imperturbable Seth, going down on his knees in time to avoid another foul shot. "There are plenty of the imps about, ain't there?"

The firing so alarmed Haverland that he desisted from his work, and sought the shelter of the wood. By this time, too, the afternoon was so far advanced that darkness had already commenced settling over the stream and wood. Crossing on the raft was now out of the question, for it would have been nothing less than suicide to have attempted it, when their enemies had given them such convincing evidence of their skill in the use of the rifle, even at a greater distance than to the middle of the stream. But the river had to be crossed for all that and the only course left, was to shift their position to some other place, build a new raft, and make another place.

There was no excuse for further delay, and the party immediately set forward. The sky again gave signs of a storm. Several rumbles of thunder were heard, but the lightning was so distant as to be of neither benefit or use to them. The sky was filled with heavy, tumultuous clouds, which rendered the darkness perfectly intense and impenetrable; and, as none of them understood a foot of the ground over which they were traveling, it may well be supposed that their progress was neither rapid nor particularly pleasant. The booming of the thunder continued, and shortly the rain commenced falling. The drops were of that big kind which are often formed in summer, and which rattle through the leaves like a shower of bullets.

"Can you look ahead, Seth?" asked Graham.

"In course I can. The darkness don't make no difference not at all to me. I can see just as well on a dark night as I can in daylight, and, what is more, I do. I should like to see me make a misstep or stumble—"

Further utterance was checked by the speaker pitching, with a loud splash, head foremost over or into something.

"You hurt, Seth?" asked Graham in alarm, yet half tempted to give way to the mirth that was convulsing those behind him.

88

"Hurt!" exclaimed the unfortunate one, scrambling to his feet, "I believe every bone of my body is broken into, and by gracious! my head is cracked, and both legs put out of joint, the left arm broke above the elbow, and the right one severed completely!"

Notwithstanding these frightful injuries, the speaker was moving about with wonderful dexterity.

"My gracious! what do you suppose I've tumbled into?" he suddenly asked.

"Into a pitfall or a hole in the ground," replied Graham. "It's my opinion, too, that it will be very easy with this noise we are making to stumble into the Mohawks' hands."

"I should think you ought to know that I didn't fall," retorted Seth angrily. "I happened to see sumthin', and I stepped forward to see if it would hold my weight. What you are laughing at, I should like to know!"

"What is it that you have stepped into?" asked Haverland.

"Why, nothing less than a boat, dragged up here by the varmints, I 'spose."

Such indeed was the case. There was a very large-sized canoe directly before them, and not a sign of the presence of others beside themselves. Not a more fortunate thing could have happened. Upon examination, the boat was found to be of unusual length and breadth, and amply sufficient to carry twenty men. It was quickly pushed back into the stream.

"Come, tumble in and we'll set sail," said Seth.

The fugitives without any hesitation entered the boat, and Seth and Haldidge, bending their shoulders to it, shoved it into the river, and sprang in as it floated away.

CHAPTER XIX.
DENOUEMENT.
The whites found in a moment that they had committed a great mistake in launching as they did. In the first place, there was not an oar in the boat, and thus, not being able to "paddle their own canoe," they were also deprived of the ability to paddle one belonging to some one else. Besides this, the river was dark

as Styx, and the whole sky and air were of the same inky blackness, and not one in the boat had the remotest idea of where they were going—whether it was to pitch over some falls, down some rapids or into the bank.

"I'm going to set down and consider which is the biggest fool, Haldidge, you or me, in starting out in this canoe which we borrowed for a short time."

So saying, Seth made his way to the stem of the canoe when he rested himself—not upon the bottom of it, as he expected, but upon something soft, which emitted a grunt audible to all, as he did so.

"My gracious! what's under me?" he exclaimed, reaching his hand down and feeling around in the dark. "A live Injin as sure as my name is Seth Jones. Ah, you copper-headed monkey!"

It was as said. An Indian had stretched out on his back with his feet dangling over the edge of the canoe, and Seth, without the faintest suspicion of his presence, had seated himself square upon his breast. As may be supposed, this was not relished at all by the startled savage, and he made several strenuous efforts to roll him off.

"Now, just lay still," commanded Seth, "for I've an idea that I can't find a more comfortable seat."

The savage was evidently so thoroughly frightened that he ceased his efforts and lay perfectly quiet and motionless.

"Have you got a real Indian here?" asked Haldidge, as he came to Seth.

"To be sure I have; just feel under me and see if I hain't."

"What you going to do with him?"

"Nothing."

"Are you going to let him off? Let's pitch him overboard."

"No, you won't, Haldidge. I've two or three good reasons for not doing such a thing. In the first place, there ain't no need of it, the poor imp hasn't hurt us; and, for all I detest his whole cowardly race, I don't believe in killing them except when they've done you some injury or are trying to. The most important reason, however, is that I don't want my seat disturbed."

"He is a cussed fool to let you sit on him that way. I'd give you a toss if I was in his place that would send you overboard."

"Not if you knew what was best for you. Thunder!"

Perhaps the Indian understood the words of the hunter. At any rate, he made an attempt to carry out his suggestion, and well nigh did it, too. Just as Seth gave vent to the exclamation recorded, he pitched headlong against Haverland, knocking him over upon his back, and falling upon him. At the same instant the savage sprang overboard and swam rapidly away in the darkness.

"That's a mean trick," said Seth, as he recovered his sitting position, "I was just setting on him to keep the rain off. Jest like the ungrateful dog!"

The attention of all was now directed to the progress of the canoe. Drifting swiftly onward through the darkness, no one knowing whither, their situation began to assume a terrible form. There was no power in their hands to guide it, and should they run into any of the trees which had caught in the bottom, or upon a rock, they would be instantly swamped. But there was no help for it and each one seated and braced himself for the shock which might come at any instant.

It was while they were proceeding in this manner, that they all heard the bottom of the canoe grate over something, then tremble for a moment, and suddenly came to a stand still. The stem swung rapidly round and commenced filling.

"Overboard men, all of you! We're sinking!" commanded Haldidge.

Each sprang into the water which was not more than two feet deep, and the canoe, thus lightened of its load, instantly freed itself and floated off in the darkness.

"Don't move till I take a few soundings," said Seth.

He naturally supposed that to reach the shore, he must take a direction at right angles with the current. A few steps showed him that he was not in the river itself, but was walking in that portion which had overflowed its banks.

"Follow on boys; we're right!" he called out.

Bushes and grass entangled their feet, and the branches overhead brushed their faces as they toiled out of the water. A few moments and they were upon solid land again. The canoe had carried them across the river, so that this troublesome task was finished.

91

"Now if we only had a fire," said Haverland.

"Yes; for Ina must be suffering."

"Oh! don't think of me!" replied the brave, little girl, cheerfully.

Seth discovered with his customary shrewdness that the storm had been very slight in this section, and the wood was comparatively dry. By removing the leaves upon the surface of the ground, there were others beneath which were perfectly free from dampness. A quantity of these were thrown in a heap, a number of twigs found among them, placed upon the top, and some larger branches piled upon these in turn. After great difficulty, Seth managed to catch a spark from his steel and tinder, and in a few moments they had a rousing, roaring genial fire.

"That's fine," said Graham. "But won't it be dangerous, Seth?"

"Let it be then, I'm bound to dry my skin to night if there's any vartue in fire."

But the Indians didn't choose to disturb them, although it was rather a reckless proceeding upon their part. It was more than probable, as Seth Jones remarked, that their pursuers had lost their trail, and would experience some difficulty in regaining and following it.

Morning at last broke upon the hungry, miserable, hopeful fugitives. As the light increased they looked about them and discovered that they had encamped at the base of a large, heavily wooded hill. It was also noticed that Haldidge, the hunter, was absent. While wondering at this, the report of his rifle was heard, and in a few moments he was seen descending the hill, bending under the weight of a half-grown deer. This was hastily dressed, several good-sized pieces skewered and cooked in the flame, and our five friends made as hearty and substantial a meal as was ever made in this world.

"Before starting upon our journey again," said Haldidge, "I want you all to go to the top of the hill here with me and see what a fine view we shall have."

"Oh! we've no time for views!" replied Seth.

"I am afraid there is little spare time," added the woodman. "But this is particularly fine, and I think you will be well pleased with it."

The hunter was so urgent that the others were finally obliged to consent. Accordingly they commenced the ascent, Haldidge leading them, and all anxiety, smiles, and expectation.

"See how you like that view!" said he, pointing off to the west.

The fugitives gazed in the direction indicated. The prospect was one indeed which, just at that time, pleased them more than could have any other in the universe; for below them about half a mile distant, was the very village toward which they had been so long making their way. It looked unusually beautiful that morning in the clear sunshine. A score of cabins nestled closely together, and the heavy smoke was lazily ascending from several chimneys, while here and there a settler could be seen moving about. At one corner of the village stood the block-house, and the gaping mouth of its swivel shone in the morning sun like burnished silver. One or two small boats were visible in the water, their ashen paddles flashing brightly as they were dipped by strong and active hands. The river down which the woodman and his wife and sisters had escaped, flowed at the foot of the village, and its windings could be traced by the eye for miles. Here and there, scattered over the country for miles could be seen an enterprising settler's cabin, resembling in the distance a tiny bee-hive.

"You haven't told me how you are pleased with the landscape?" said the hunter.

"Ah, Haldidge, you know better than to ask that question," replied Haverland in a shaking voice. "Thank God that He has been so merciful to us!"

They now commenced descending the hill. Not a word was exchanged between them, for their hearts were too full for attendance. A strange spell seemed to have come over Seth Jones. At sight of the village, he had suddenly become thoughtful and silent, refusing even to answer a question. His head was bent down. Evidently his mind was engrossed upon some all-absorbing subject. Several times he sighed deeply, and pressed his hand to his heart, as though the tumultuous throbbing there pained him. The expression of his face was wonderfully changed. That quizzing, comical look was entirely gone, while wrinkles at the eyebrows and base of the nose could be seen no more. His face appeared positively handsome. It was a wonderful metamorphosis, and the question passed around unexpressed: "is that Seth Jones?"

All at once, he seemed to become sensible that the eyes of others were upon him, and that he had forgotten himself. That old, peculiar expression came back to his face, and a few steps of the old straddling gait were taken, and Seth Jones was himself again!

The sentinels in the block-house had discovered and recognized the fugitives, and when they arrived at the palisade which surrounded the village, there were numbers waiting to receive them.

"I will see you all again!" said Haldidge, separating from the others and passing toward the upper end of the settlement.

After pausing a few moments to answer the inquiries of their friends, Haverland led the way toward the cabin where he had left his wife and sister. Here he found the good settlers had erected and presented him with a house. As he stepped softly to the door, intending to give his wife a playful surprise, she met him. With a low cry of joy, she sprang forward and was held in his arms, and the next instant she and Ina were clasped together and weeping.

"Thank Heaven! thank Heaven! Oh, my dear, dear child, I thought you lost forever."

Graham and Seth stood respectfully to one side for a few moments. The latter cleared his throat several times and brushed his arm across his forehead in a suspicious manner. As the mother regained herself, she turned and recognized Graham, and greeted him warmly.

"And you, too," she said, taking Seth's hand and looking up into his face, "have been more than a friend to us. May Heaven reward you, for we never can."

"There! by gracious! don't say no more!—boohoo! ahem! I believe I've caught a cold being so exposed to the night air!"

But it was no use; the tears would come; and Seth, for a few seconds, wept like a baby, yet smiled even through his tears. They all entered the house.

"Our first duty is to thank God for his mercy. Let us all do it," said the woodman.

All sank devoutly upon their knees, joining in fervent thanksgiving to the great Being who had shown his goodness to them in such a marvellous manner.

The settlers, with true politeness of heart, forebore to intrude until they judged the family were desirous of seeing them. After they had arisen from their knees, Mary, the sister of Haverland, entered. Graham chanced to glance at Seth that moment, and was startled at the emotion he exhibited. He flushed scarlet, and trembled painfully, but, by a strong effort recovered himself in time to greet her. She thanked him again and commenced conversing, when she saw that he was embarrassed and ill at ease. A flash of suspicion crossed her fine calm face, and it became pale and flushed by turns. What a riot emotion was making in her heart only she herself knew:—her face soon became passive and pensive; and a pathos gleamed from her sad eyes which sent Seth quickly out of doors to commune with the mysteries of his own thoughts.

The cabin was crowded until near midnight with congratulating friends. Prominent among these, was the man who officiated in the capacity of minister for the settlement. He was a portly, genial, good-natured man, of the Methodist persuasion, and a preacher for the times—one who could plow, reap, chop wood, and lead the settlers against their foes when he deemed it necessary, or preach and practice the gospel before them.

It was a glad—a happy reunion—a night that was long remembered.

Just one week after the reunion, the little party was seated in Haverland's home, composed of Ina, Seth Jones, the woodman, Mrs. Haverland, and Mary. Seth sat in one corner conversing with Ina, while the other three were also together. There was a happy look upon each face. Even the sweet melancholy beauty of Mary was lightened up by a smile. She was beautiful—queenly so. Her hair, black as night, was gathered behind, as if to restrain its tendency to curl; but in spite of this, a refractory one was constantly intruding itself. A faint color was visible in her cheeks, and her blue eye had in it something of a gleam of the common joy and peace.

Seth had remained most of the time with the woodman. Several times he had asked Mary Haverland to walk with him, and yet, upon each occasion, when about to start, he become painfully nervous and begged to be excused. And then his language was so different at times. Often he would converse with words so polished and well chosen, as to show unmistakably that he was a scholar. Perhaps the reader has noticed this discrepancy in his conversations. It attracted attention, and strengthened many in their belief that for some unknown reason he was playing a part.

At the present time, there was a nervousness in his manner; and, although he was holding a playful conversation with Ina, his eyes were constantly wandering to the face of Mary Haverland.

"And so you and Graham are going to be married to-morrow night?" he asked.

"You know, Seth, that we are. How many times are you going to ask me?"

95

"Do you love him?" he asked, looking her steadily in the face.

"What a question! I have always loved him, and always will."

"That's right; then marry him, for if man ever loved woman, he loves you! And, Alf; while I think of it," he spoke in a louder tone, "what has that big, red-haired fellow been hanging around here so much, for the last day or two?"

"You will have to ask Mary," laughed the woodman.

"Oh! I understand; there'll be two weddings to-morrow night, eh? That's so, Mary?"

"Not that I know of; I have no expectation of becoming a wife for any one."

"Hain't eh? Why the man seems to love you. Why don't you marry him?"

"I am afraid Mary will never marry," said Haverland. "She has rejected all offers, though many were from very desirable men."

"Queer! I never heard of such a case."

"Her love was buried long ago," replied Haverland, in a lower tone, to Seth.

After a moment's silence, Seth arose, took his chair, and seated himself beside her. She did not look at him, nor did any one else. He sat a moment; then whispered:—

"Mary?"

She started. Her eyes flashed like meteors in his face a moment; then she turned as pale as death, and would have fallen from her chair, had not Seth caught her in his arms. Haverland looked up in amazement; the whole family were riveted in wonder. Seth looked up from the face of the fainting woman, and smiled as he said: "She is mine, forever!"

"Merciful heaven! Eugene Morton!" exclaimed Haverland, starting to his feet.

"It is so!" said the one addressed.

"Have you risen from the dead?"

"I have risen to life, Alf, but have never been with the dead."

Instead of the weak, squeaking tone which had heretofore characterized his speech, was now a rich, mellow bass, whose tones startled Mary into life again. She raised her head, but he who held her, would not permit her to arise. He pressed her fervently to his bosom. The ecstasy of that moment, only the angels in heaven could fathom.

Haldidge and Graham entered, and the man in his true character, arose to his feet—a tall, dignified, graceful, imposing person.

"Where is Seth?" asked Graham, not noticing the apparent stranger.

"Here is what you have heretofore supposed to be that individual," laughed the person before him, enjoying greatly their astonishment.

"Seth, truly, but not Seth, either," exclaimed they both, with astonishment written on their faces.

"With a few words," he commenced, "all will be plain to you. I need not tell you, friends, that my character, since my advent among you, has been an assumed one. Seth Jones is a myth, and to my knowledge, no such person ever existed. My real name is Eugene Morton. Ten years ago, Mary Haverland and I pledged our love to each other. We were to be married in one year; but, when a few months of that time had elapsed, the Revolutionary War broke out, and a call was made upon our little village, in New Hampshire, for volunteers. I had no desire, nor right to refuse. Our little company proceeded to Massachusetts, where the war was then raging. In a skirmish, a few days after the battle of Bunker Hill, I was dangerously wounded, and was left with a farmer by the wayside. I sent word by one of my comrades to Mary, that I was disabled, but hoped to see her in a short time. The bearer of that message probably was killed, for it is certain, my words never reached her; though a very different report, did. We had a man in our company, who was a lover of Mary's. Knowing of my misfortune, he sent her word that I was killed. When I rejoined my company, a few months after, I learned that this man had deserted. A suspicion that he had returned home, impelled me to obtain leave of absence to visit my native place. I there learned that Haverland, with his wife and sister, had left the village for the West. One of my friends informed me that this deserter had gone with them, and, it was understood, would marry Mary. I could not doubt the truth of this report, and, for a time, I feared I should commit suicide. To soften this great sorrow, I returned at once, joined our company, and plunged into every

97

battle that I possibly could. I often purposely exposed myself to danger, soliciting death rather than life. In the winter of 1776, I found myself under General Washington, at Trenton; I had crossed the Delaware with him, and, by the time it was fairly light, we were engaged in a desperate fight with the Hessians. In the very heat of the battle, the thought suddenly came to me, that the story of Mary's marriage was untrue. Singularly enough, when the battle was over, I did not think any more of it. But in the midst of the following engagement at Princeton, the same thought came to me again, and haunted me from that time, until the close of the war. I determined to seek out Mary. All that I could learn, was, that Haverland had emigrated 'out this way.' If she had married the deserter, I knew it was under a firm belief that I was dead. Consequently I had no right to pain her by my presence. For this reason, I assumed a disguise. I discolored my now long untamed hair. It so changed my whole appearance, that I hardly knew myself. My youthful color was now changed into the bronze of war, and sorrow had wrought its changes. It was not strange then, that any old friend should not know me, particularly when I could so successfully personate the 'Green Mountain Boy,' in voice and manner. My identity was perfectly secure, I knew, from detection. I came in this section, and after a long and persevering hunt, one day I found Haverland cutting in the wood. I introduced myself to him as Seth Jones. I found Mary. The report which had reached me of her marriage was false, she was still true to her first love! I should have made myself known then, had not the danger which threatened Haverland, come upon him almost immediately. As his family were then tormented by the fate of Ina, I thought my recognition would only serve to embarrass and distract their actions. Besides, I felt some amusement in the part I was playing, and often enjoyed the speculation I created, by giving you, as it were, a glimpse now and then into my real nature, I varied my actions and language, on purpose to increase your wonder." He here paused and smiled, as if at the recollection of his numerous ludicrous escapades. He continued: "I have little more to add. I congratulate you, Graham, on the prize you have won. You are to be married to-morrow night. Mary, will you not marry me at the same time?"

"Yes," replied the radiant woman, placing her hands in his. "You have my hand now, as you have had my heart through all these long, sorrowing years."

Morton kissed her forehead tenderly.

"Now, congratulate me," said he, with a beaming face.

And they gathered around him, and such shaking of hands, and such greetings, we venture to say, were never seen before. Our friends experienced some difficulty at first, in believing that Seth Jones was gone forever. They even felt some regrets that his pleasing, eccentric face had passed away; but, they had gained in his place, a handsome, noble-hearted man, of whom they were all proud.

The next day was spent in preparations for the great double wedding that was to take place that evening. Messengers were sent up and down the river, and back into the woods, there was not a settler within twenty miles, who had not been invited. At nightfall, the company began to collect. Some came in boats, some on horseback, and others on foot. A double wedding rarely took place in the backwoods, and while this occasion was too full of romance to be slighted by any, old or young.

When the lights were produced in the woodman's house, there was a motley assemblage without and within. You could have heard old and middle-aged men talking about the prospect of the crops, and looking up to the sky, and wisely predicating the probabilities of a change in the weather, or discussing, in anxious tones, the state of feeling among the Indians along the frontier; you could have heard—as they would be termed now-a-days—"gawky" young men as sagely discoursing upon the same subjects, venturing a playful thrust now and then, at one of their number about some "Alminy," or "Serapheemy," sweetheart.

The woodman's house had been much enlarged for the occasion. A long shed amply sufficient to contain all the guests, was built alongside, and connecting with it. After participating in a bountiful meal in this, the tables were removed, and preparation made for the marriage.

A sudden hush fell upon the assemblage. All eyes turned toward the door, through which Eugene Morton and Edward Graham, each with his affianced leaning upon his arm entered.

"Ain't they purty?"

"Don't they look bootiful?"

"Golly! if they ain't some, then there's no use in talking!"

Such and similar were the whispered remarks of admiration at the couple. Mary Haverland was dressed in a plain, light colored dress, without any ornament, except a single white rose in her hair, which now fell in dark masses over her shoulders. Her beauty was of the truly regal type. She was very happy, yet seemed as if in a world of her own.

Horton was clad in gray homespun, which well became his graceful form. His whole appearance was that of the gentleman, which he was—a brave soldier, a true-hearted man.

Ina, the sweet, young heroine, was fascinating. Her dress was of the purest white. Her curls clustered around her shoulders, and were confined at the temples by a simple wreath of blue violets. There was a contrast between Ina and Mary, and yet it would have been a difficult task to have judged which was the most beautiful—the pure, queenly, trusting woman, or the purity and innocence of the young maiden. Graham was a worthy participant in the drama, and pleased all by his goodness and intelligence.

In a few moments, a portly gentleman, with a white neckcloth, and all aglow with smiles, entered the room. Morton and Mary arose and stood before him, and amid the most perfect silence the ceremony commenced. The questions were put and answered in a firm voice, audible to every one in the room.

"What God hath joined together let not man put asunder."

And every voice said "Amen!" as they reseated themselves.

Haldidge, who had stood as groomsman to Morton, now signaled with a quiet smile for Graham to take his position. The young hero did, and Ina, blushing deeply, and leaning on the arm of her bridemaid, followed, and the ceremony commenced.

While this was proceeding, an interesting affair was occurring on the opposite end of the room. A large, bony, red-faced young man, sat holding and squeezing the hand of a bouncing buxom girl, and indulging in several expressive remarks.

"I swow, if they don't look purty. Wonder how the gal feels?"

"Why happy, of course," replied his companion.

"By jingo, I bet he does; I know I would."

"You would what?"

"Feel glorious if I was in his place."

"What! marrying Ina Haverland?"

100

"No—I mean—ahem!—why, somebody else—that is—yes, somebody else."

"Who else do you mean?" asked the girl, looking him steadily in the face.

"Why—ahem!—why, you! darn it, now you know, don't you?"

"Sh! Don't talk so loud, Josiah, or they'll hear you."

"S'posen you was in her place, Sal; how would you feel?"

"Ain't you ashamed of yourself?" she asked reprovingly.

"No, darnation, I don't care. Say, Sal, how would you feel?"

"Do you mean if I was standing out there with you, and the minister talking so to us?"

"Yes—yes; why don't you tell me?"

"You know well enough, Josiah, without asking me no such question."

Josiah commenced meditating. Some desperate scheme was evidently troubling him, for he scratched his head and then his knees, and then laughed, and exclaimed to himself, "I'll do it, by George!" Then turning toward the girl, he said:

"Sal, let's you and I get married, won't you?"

"Why, Josiah?" and she hung her head and blushed charmingly.

"Come, Sal, the old folks won't care. Let's do it, won't you?"

"Oh, Josiah!" she continued, growing nervous and fidgety.

"Come, say quick, for the dominie is near done, and he'll go home. Say yes; Sal, do."

"Oh, dear! oh, my stars!—YES!"

"Good, by jingo! Hurry up there, Mr. Preacher."

At this point, the good minister ceased his benediction upon the couples, and their friends commenced crowding around them. The minister started, not

101

to go home, but to leave the room for a moment, when Josiah noticed it, and fearing that he was going called out:

"Say, squire—you, dominie, I mean, just wait, won't you here's another job for you."

"Ah! I am glad to hear it!" laughed the minister, turning round. "Are you the happy man?"

"Wal, I reckon so, and I cac'late as how, Sal Clayton there is the happy gal."

All eyes were turned toward the speaker, and he stood their smiles unflinchingly. His face was of a fiery red, and a large, flowing necktie hung disregarded over his breast.

"Go in, Josiah; that's you!" exclaimed several patting him on the shoulder.

"Get out all of you, till I'm through. Come up here, Sal; no use scroochin' now."

The females bore the blushing one forward, until she was near enough for Josiah to get hold of her hand.

"Now go ahead, squire—you—minister, I mean, and don't be too thundering long about it, for I want to get married most terribly."

The company gave way, and the two stepped forward, and in a few moments were pronounced man and wife. When Josiah saluted his bride, the smack was a telling one, and the congratulations of Morton and Graham were nothing to those which were showered upon the happy man.

Now the sport commenced. An old ranger suddenly made his appearance, bearing a violin under his arm—"a reg'lar old cremony," as he termed it. The word was given to "make ready for the dance!" The old folks disappeared and entered the house, where, with the minister, they indulged in conversation, story-telling, nuts, apples, and cider.

The fiddler coiled himself upon the top of a box, and commenced twisting the screws of his instrument, and thumbing the strings. The operation of "tuning" was evidently a painful one, for it was noticed that at each turn of the screw, he shut one eye and twisted his mouth.

The violin was at length tuned, the bow was given two or three sweeps across a lump of rosin, and then drawn across the strings, as if it said "attention!" As the couples were forming, the violinist slid partly down off the box, so that one foot could beat upon the sanded floor, and then, giving his head a jerk backward, struck up a reel that fairly set every heart dancing. The floor was immediately filled with the young folks. Tall, strapping fellows plunged around the room, like skeletons of india-rubber, their legs bowed out, and sometimes tripping over each other. Rousing, solid girls bounded around, up and down like pots of jelly, and "all went merry as a marriage-bell."

By and by the old folks made their appearance "just to see the boys and gals enjoy themselves." The fiddler at this moment shot off on the "Devil's Dream." A timid elderly lady stepped up to him, and touching him softly on the shoulder, asked:

"Isn't that a profane tune?"

"No, it's Old Hundredth with variations—don't bother me," replied the performer, relieving his mouth of a quantity of tobacco juice at the same time.

"Supposing we try it for a moment, aunt Hannah," said the minister with a sly look.

The two stepped out on the floor, the fiddler commenced another tune, and they disappeared in the whirling mass. In a few moments nearly all of the old folks who had come just to "see them a minute," followed, and the way in which several elderly gentlemen and ladies executed some of the reels of a half-century's memory, was a lesson to the younger folks.

The company kept up their revelry until far beyond midnight. But by and by they commenced withdrawing. It was proposed by several to visit the different bridegrooms in bed, but fortunately the good taste of the others prevailed, and they departed quietly homeward.

Slumber, with the exception of the sentinels at the block-house, fell upon the village. Perhaps the Indians had no wish to break in upon such a happy settlement, for they made no demonstration through the night. Sweetly and peacefully they all slept; sweetly and peacefully they entered upon life's duties on the morrow; and sweetly and peacefully these happy settlers ascend and went down the hillside of life.

Made in the USA
Coppell, TX
04 November 2022

85738992R10062